DATE DUE AUG 0 5

9 2 0 0			
OCT 26 '05			
GAYLORD			PRINTED IN U.S.A.

Daddy, He Wrote

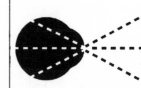 This Large Print Book carries the
Seal of Approval of N.A.V.H.

Daddy, He Wrote

Jill Limber

Thorndike Press • Waterville, Maine

Published in 2005 by arrangement with Harlequin Books S.A.

Thorndike Press® Large Print Romance.

The tree indicium is a trademark of Thorndike Press.

The text of this Large Print edition is unabridged.
Other aspects of the book may vary from the original edition.

Set in 16 pt. Plantin by Minnie B. Raven.

Printed in the United States on permanent paper.

Library of Congress Cataloging-in-Publication Data

Limber, Jill.
    Daddy, he wrote / by Jill Limber.
        p. cm.
    ISBN 0-7862-7657-6 (lg. print : hc : alk. paper)
    1. Authors — Fiction.   2. Single mothers — Fiction.
3. Country life — Fiction.   4. Housekeepers — Fiction.
5. Widows — Fiction.   6. Large type books.   I. Title.
PS3612.I49D33 2005
    813'.6—dc22   2005005558

To Teresa, the best kind of friend.
No matter what, I know I can count on you!

As the Founder/CEO of NAVH, the only national health agency solely devoted to those who, although not totally blind, have an eye disease which could lead to serious visual impairment, I am pleased to recognize Thorndike Press* as one of the leading publishers in the large print field.

Founded in 1954 in San Francisco to prepare large print textbooks for partially seeing children, NAVH became the pioneer and standard setting agency in the preparation of large type.

Today, those publishers who meet our standards carry the prestigious "Seal of Approval" indicating high quality large print. We are delighted that Thorndike Press is one of the publishers whose titles meet these standards. We are also pleased to recognize the significant contribution Thorndike Press is making in this important and growing field.

Lorraine H. Marchi, L.H.D.
Founder/CEO
NAVH

* Thorndike Press encompasses the following imprints: Thorndike, Wheeler, Walker and Large Print Press.

Blacksmith Farm To Do List:

1) Make Mr. Miller breakfast

2) Wash Emma's bibs and blankets

3) Stop thinking about sexy new boss!

4) Feed the horses, the cat and the dog

5) Wash kitchen floor

6) Stop thinking about sexy new boss!!!

7) Buy groceries

8) Stop thinking about sexy new boss!!!!

Chapter One

Trish dropped the box of books she'd just begun to unpack and grabbed the telephone before the ringing could wake three-month-old Emma. If the baby hadn't been in the room, she'd let the machine pick up. She'd been dodging phone calls for three months.

Heart pounding, she said, "Hello, Blacksmith Farm."

"Is this the housekeeper?" an arrogant-sounding female voice asked.

Trish answered, knowing this could be the call that ended her job. If that happened, she and Emma would be homeless. "Yes. This is Trish —"

The impatient caller cut her off. "This is Joyce Sommers. I'm Mr. Miller's business manager."

Mr. Miller was the new owner of Blacksmith Farm. Trish waited through the woman's dramatic pause, wanting to make a sarcastic comment but knowing that would not be the wisest step, considering her circumstances.

"I have a list of things that need to be

done before Mr. Miller arrives."

Trish sat down at the desk, fearing her shaky legs might not support her. If she was getting instructions she still had the job. On a giddy wave of relief she started scribbling furiously to get down everything Ms. Sommers wanted accomplished in the next two days.

She assured Ms. Sommers that everything would be done before Mr. Miller visited, then the woman hung up without even a goodbye.

With a shaking hand, Trish replaced the receiver and stared at the telephone. Relief spread through her, and she felt the knot of tension between her shoulder blades ease a bit.

Despite her worry, Trish supposed she shouldn't be surprised. The caretaker came with the property, just like the furnishings and the animals. The old owners had sold everything, lock, stock and barrel, literally.

If she was lucky, the new owner would spend as little time here as the old owner had.

She glanced over at Emma, sound asleep on her back in a wash basket lined with a quilt, her tiny hands curled into fists and her mouth making little sucking motions.

Trish's heart swelled with love every time she looked at her daughter.

In their short marriage, Billy had been a miserable husband and an indifferent father, but he'd given her Emma. Part of Trish would thank him forever for that.

Through the window of the study, just past the barn, she could see the cracked shingles of the old stone farmhouse that went with the caretaker's job. It had no heat except the fireplace; the electrical wiring was ancient and undependable; and the water pump didn't work when the power was out. She loved every square leaky, drafty inch of it. It was hers, the first place she had ever been able to call home.

Trish emptied the box she'd been working to unpack before Ms. Sommers's call, and realized all the books were multiple copies of the ones written by the new owner.

She looked at the floor-to-ceiling bookcases on the west wall, trying to decide where to put one of each of Mr. Miller's books. He'd be proud of his work and want them at eye level, she decided, where people would see them when they came in the room.

She carried an armload to the shelves.

This was her favorite room in the house. She loved to read.

She shelved a copy of each volume and ran her fingers down the spines to make sure they were aligned. The rest she stored in a cupboard.

What would it be like to be rich and live in a house like this and have enough time to read every day? In her dreams she pictured Emma and herself in a big, safe, cozy house like this. She'd have a housekeeper and a gardener. She'd have time to play with Emma whenever she wanted, and after she tucked Emma into bed at night, she'd curl up in the big flowered chair in the front room and read until bedtime.

Trish sighed at her own foolishness as she dusted the shelves. He must be very smart to write these books. She'd read all of them. Ian Miller was one of the most popular authors today. He hit the *New York Times* best-seller list with each new book.

She pulled out a volume of his latest release and studied the black-and-white picture of him on the dust jacket. Incredibly handsome, he looked more like a movie star than a writer. He was dressed in a tux and had a glass of champagne in his hand.

Trish smiled. He wouldn't spend much time here. She loved the farm and this wonderful old restored house, but it was way out in the middle of the Pennsylvania countryside, miles from his home in Philadelphia and the glittering New York life someone like Ian Miller would be used to.

He'd be like the previous owner. He and his wife said they wanted a retreat from the stressful life in Manhattan, but they rarely used the farm.

They'd stocked the place with horses and a cow, then they'd split their time between a flat in London and a penthouse apartment in New York.

Trish would never understand how rich people's minds worked.

She traced her finger over the picture of the elegant-looking man and smiled.

No, he wouldn't spend time here.

She and Emma would have their little stone house.

Ian Miller considered heaving the telephone against the wall in frustration. "Joyce, I thought I made it clear I wasn't doing any more publicity appearances or book signings for a while."

Her cool, steady voice, a sound that he was starting to hate, made a falsely sympathetic murmur. "I know, Ian, but you

13

agreed to this tour before the holidays. Before you made that ultimatum."

Her tone told him just what she thought of his warning.

Ian hadn't remembered agreeing to any such thing, but when he was on deadline he knew he sometimes said what Joyce wanted to hear just to get her off the telephone. "When do I leave?"

"A car will pick you up tomorrow morning at seven."

He groaned. He'd planned to work all day tomorrow, even though he knew what he'd been writing lately was worthless and would never end up in a book. He'd been promoted as a "boy wonder" with his first book, had phenomenal success with all his subsequent releases and now was in danger of burning out before he turned thirty.

He'd never hit such a slump in his writing career. It was driving him crazy. He felt a compulsion to write a different kind of book, but the effort was going nowhere and frustrating the hell out of him.

He turned his attention back to Joyce, who was droning away about some party she'd attended. Some party where *he* should have been, to meet people.

He cut her off. "How long will I be gone?" He really needed to fire her, then he wouldn't have to do tours and book signings.

He probably would have let her go by now if they hadn't had a history. The affair was over, but he felt guilty about firing her. He didn't want her to think that because he was no longer having sex with her he had no further need of her.

"Ian?"

Obviously, he hadn't been paying attention. "What?"

"I did schedule in a stop at the farm." He could hear the disdain in her voice. Joyce thought the farm was a bad idea and had been very vocal about it.

That almost made the trip sound good. He rubbed at the tension headache building up between his eyes.

"Okay. I'll be ready at seven."

He hung up and stared out his penthouse window at the streets. The trees had all lost their leaves, and he could see people, hundreds of them, bundled against the cold, walking their dogs, their children and each other.

Ian had no use for other people. He'd discovered early on that a fair number of his fellow city dwellers bordered on crazy.

A month ago he'd been followed home from a lunch with his editor by two middle-aged women who had barged into his building behind him, sidestepped the doorman and insisted they wanted to see his apartment.

Just last week he'd found a young woman sitting on the hood of his car in the secured underground parking garage in his building, holding a copy of his latest book. Wearing a very short skirt and top that showed her navel, complete with a diamond stud, she'd made it very clear she was interested in more than an autograph.

Ian cursed the day Joyce had talked him into letting his publisher put his picture on the dust jacket of his book. They'd just started their affair and she'd been very persuasive. Now he supposed removing the picture from future covers would be like closing the barn door after the horse had escaped, but he craved anonymity.

He wanted so badly to be out of the city where he'd grown up. Aside from insane fans, he was tired of the social whirl and the constant interruptions. He wanted to be alone, at the farm he'd just bought. He was sure that in the solitude of the Pennsylvania countryside he would rediscover his creativity.

He'd spent a total of an hour there, inspecting the property. It had felt so right to him, he'd bought it on the spot. He loved everything about it. The quiet, the isolation, the fact that aside from an old stone farmhouse where the caretakers lived, you couldn't even see another house.

The main house, a restored plank house, was plenty big, with its warm, inviting and comfortable interior.

The whole place was obviously well cared for. He hadn't met the people who worked there, but if they stayed out of Ian's way and did their jobs, Ian didn't care if he ever met them.

He'd always needed complete quiet and solitude to write. Philadelphia was becoming impossible. Not only did fans hound him, but his parents demanded he be a part of their busy society circle, as if he were some kind of trophy they'd acquired.

He'd considered moving to New York to be closer to his publisher and editor, but that was as bad as Philadelphia. He was tired of being pressured to show up at the important parties, invited because of his fame. No one wanted to *know* him, they just wanted to be seen with him.

The more he declined what Joyce described as the "significant invitations," the more popular he became.

The business end of his life was no

better. He'd hired an army of people to take care of things. Joyce, his agent, a property manager, an accountant, and they just seemed to complicate his life instead of freeing him up.

He wanted to be able to write in peace and quiet, live an uncomplicated life with no interruptions. He wanted what Thoreau had sought, his own Walden Pond.

No entanglements.

Maybe then he could get his old spark back and write a decent book to give to his publisher. He had a deadline looming, and nothing he was willing to show anyone, especially his editor.

He closed the program on his laptop and went to pack, his spirits lifting at the thought he would at least get to stop at the farm.

When he returned home he'd have the rest of the things he wanted to take with him packed and shipped. If the place turned out to be as conducive to work as he hoped, he'd think about putting his apartment up for sale.

Chapter Two

Trish was working in the barn when she heard the car coming up the driveway that led only to the farm.

It couldn't be him, not yet, she thought frantically, looking down at her filthy clothes.

He wasn't scheduled to arrive for three hours. Thank goodness she'd finished getting the house ready this morning.

She dumped her shovelful of manure into the wheelbarrow and yanked off her gloves. Wiping her hands on the rag stuffed in her pocket, she walked over to glance into the basket on the workbench where Emma had just fallen asleep. She tucked the warm blanket securely around her daughter and kissed her forehead with a brush of her lips.

"Finish your nap, sweetheart," she whispered. "Mama will be just outside."

Emma always slept for at least an hour this time of the day, but Trish hated to leave her alone, even though she'd be only a short distance away.

She grabbed Tollie's collar and shut him in the goat pen. The old blind mutt didn't have the sense to stay out from under the wheels of the car.

Running her fingers through her short hair, she wished she'd had time to shower and change before she met the famous Ian Miller.

When she stepped out into the thin winter sunshine, the limousine was making a turn in the area between the barn and the main house. The car's windows were tinted with such dark glass she couldn't see the occupants of the car.

The car pulled to a stop about twenty feet from her, and a middle-aged driver in a rumpled suit jumped out and opened the rear door.

Ian Miller stepped out, his attention on the house. Her breath caught in her throat. The man was devastatingly handsome, much more than his photograph had shown.

He paid no attention to her. Either he hadn't seen her or he was as rude as his business manager.

She pushed aside a feeling of disappointment. It didn't matter, she told herself. The less he noticed her the better if she was going to be able to pull off her plan to keep both jobs.

His inattention gave her a chance to collect herself and study him. He was tall, over six feet, with thick, well-cut black hair.

His clothes were beautiful. He wore a gray-and-navy tweed jacket over broad shoulders, a navy turtleneck sweater and gray wool slacks, perfectly tailored to fit to his slim hips. His leather shoes looked costly and new.

Even from where she stood she could see he had strong square hands with clean, well-tended fingernails and an expensive-looking gold wristwatch.

The man was elegant. She'd never met a man who looked as classy as Ian Miller.

Self-consciously Trish smoothed the front of the flannel shirt that hung to her knees, wishing her boots weren't caked with manure. She wore Billy's clothes when she was working, to save wear and tear on what little wardrobe she had.

The limousine driver spotted her and tipped his hat. He cleared his throat, and Mr. Miller turned to him, one eyebrow quirked in question.

Then he looked past the driver and saw her. He went very still, his face etched with a brief flash of surprise, then his expression went blank as he looked her up and down. She noticed he had gorgeous blue eyes. The shade of blue the sky turned at twilight, deep and rich.

Trish sucked in a breath. This was it. She needed to appear competent to keep her job. She was good at bluffing. When you grew up the way she had, it was a necessary survival skill.

She plastered a smile on her face and took a step toward him. She didn't miss the flash of suspicion that crossed his handsome face.

"Mr. Miller?"

He hesitated, then nodded reluctantly, as if he'd been caught by someone he didn't care to see. She didn't have time to wonder at his curious reaction to her.

Nervously she smiled again, wondering if he could see how strained the expression felt on her face. She stopped about ten feet from the car and him. "I'm Trish Ryan."

"You're the housekeeper?" His expression relaxed a little but remained guarded as he nodded. "Ms. Ryan, I'm pleased to meet you." His voice was deep, mellow and had a faint upper-class sound to it.

Trish didn't think he looked pleased at

all, but she had the sense not to mention it. "Welcome to Blacksmith Farm."

"Thank you," he replied politely.

His apparent lack of interest in her helped to put her at ease. "Can I show you the house?" she asked, hoping the answer would be no.

She wouldn't leave Emma alone in the barn, and if he said yes she'd have to go and get her daughter. She'd rather he didn't know about Emma. Her gut told her Emma was a complication she should avoid explaining on their first meeting.

He looked down at her boots and shook his head. Trish felt a spurt of relief. If she were him she wouldn't want her boots in the house, either.

Then he looked beyond her with a scowl. She turned and saw he was looking at the paddock beside the barn where two of the three horses were placidly grazing. Max stood with his head hanging over the fence, watching her. He was more like a dog than a horse, following her with his curious three-legged gait whenever she worked around the barn or paddock.

"Didn't Ms. Sommers tell you to get rid of the animals?" he asked curtly.

Trish nodded. "Yes. The cow has already been sold to the neighbors. The dealer who's taking the horses is coming to-morrow morning."

She never could figure out why the former owner had wanted a cow. They never even drank milk the few times they stayed at the farm. Rich people baffled her with their lack of sense.

Mr. Miller nodded and turned his attention back to the house. He had a marvelous profile, very strong and masculine.

Trish stood there, impatiently waiting for him to say something. She needed to get back to Emma. And to work.

A horse whinnied loudly from the paddock. She recognized Max's voice. He was a big baby, but she really would miss him.

Trish pushed the sentimental thought away. What did she need with a three-legged horse?

She was exhausted caring for her daughter, the house, the animals and the property. It would make her life easier if she didn't have to maintain the animals, especially now that cold winter weather had set in.

She wouldn't miss milking the cow twice a day, but she already regretted not having fresh milk. She'd learned to make butter and had been going to try to make cheese. Having the cow had saved on groceries and reduced the hassle of taking the bus to the supermarket as often.

A cold breeze raised goose bumps on her arms, and she glanced at the barn. Even though Emma was all bundled up and snug in her basket, it was still chilly.

She couldn't figure out how to speed up his visit without being too obvious, so she decided to get a business detail out of the way.

She cleared her throat, and he turned away from his perusal of the house. "I assume you want the money from the sale of the animals deposited in the household account?"

Mr. Miller shrugged. "I suppose. Do you keep the accounts?"

Trish nodded. She kept painfully detailed records of all the money she deposited and spent out of the Blacksmith Farm account.

She had to buy more fuel oil soon and pay the men who were working in the orchard this week.

"Fine. If you need more operating money, I'll give you the name of my accountant. He'll check your records and see you get what you need."

The horses should bring a great deal of money at auction, so she wouldn't have to ask for quite a while.

She was glad to hear him say he was turning the financial dealings over to an accountant. That was what someone who didn't plan to spend much time here would do.

He turned back to the house, staring at the exterior. She suppressed a shiver and wondered what he was doing, just standing out here in the cold, looking. "Are you sure I can't show you around?"

He seemed to come out of his trance. "No. I'll go in by myself. Is the house locked?" Absently he fished around in his pocket as if he could come up with a key. She wondered if he had one.

"No. Both the front and back are open." As soon as the words were out of her mouth, she realized her mistake. She braced herself for a rebuke for leaving his property unlocked.

Way out here in the country it seemed perfectly reasonable to her to leave the doors open during the day.

He smiled, as if it amused him. "Unlocked," he muttered. "Good."

It was the first halfway pleasant expression she'd seen on his face.

He turned and walked toward the house, his leather shoes crunching over the gravel drive. His long-legged stride ate up the ground.

She watched him walk away then glanced over at the limousine driver, who smiled at her and shrugged. She waited until Mr. Miller disappeared inside the house to speak to the driver.

She felt awkward asking the question, as if she were invading Mr. Miller's privacy, but she needed to know. "How long is he going to be here?"

The driver looked at his watch. "Not long if he wants to be at his next destination on time."

Trish heaved a sigh of relief and smiled at the man. She was prepared to fix Mr. Miller dinner if he stayed, but she still had a lot of work to do. He was the new owner and possibly the most handsome man Trish had ever encountered, but for her sake, the less time he spent here the better.

"I need to finish up in the barn. Will you give me a tap on the horn if he wants to see me before you leave?"

"Sure thing." He gave her a little salute and climbed back in the car.

Smart man. It was really getting cold. She turned and hurried back to the barn. When she was working she didn't notice the cold, but just standing there she'd felt it cut right through her clothes.

Trish peeked into Emma's basket at her sleeping baby and felt the surge of love that always took her by surprise. She'd never been in love before, and the warm feelings brought tears to her eyes. She watched her perfect little face, composed in sleep. Emma was the only purely good thing that had ever happened to her.

She kissed the smooth cheek, inhaling the wonderful scent of clean baby and whispered, "This is going to work, darling girl, I just know it is."

Ian looked out the window of the front room of his new home and watched Trish finish her conversation with his driver, then turn and run into the barn.

When he'd first noticed her he'd thought she was a teenager. Then a breeze had kicked up and plastered her shirt against her body, letting him know there was a woman's shape under all that ugly flannel.

She couldn't be much over five feet tall, and she looked as if she was wearing her father's clothes. He hadn't missed the fact that her breasts had looked almost too large for her slender frame.

As lovely as her figure appeared to be, it had been her eyes that had caught his attention. Big and blue and too old looking for her young face. Trish had sad eyes. Sad and a little wary.

He found himself wondering about the appealing little waif with tousled blond curls. Why would a woman who looked that young have such old eyes? Why had he even remembered her name?

He was terrible with names. Usually he had to meet people several times before he remembered them. He'd had the same doorman for a year and still couldn't recall the man's name.

What was he doing, spending time thinking about his housekeeper? She was definitely not the type of woman he was usually attracted to.

A little disgusted with himself, Ian turned away from the window and looked around the front room, trying to shake off his odd fascination with a woman he barely knew.

The interior of the house was as homey and well kept as he remembered. The woman might look young, but she was doing a good job.

He vaguely remembered Joyce mentioning the caretakers came with the farm and lived in the old stone house on the property. So did that mean she was half of a couple?

He told himself it was only curiosity, the way his writer's brain worked. He asked himself questions and created scenarios to go with what he saw.

Yeah, right, he thought. Had he asked himself any questions about the limo driver? No.

He reminded himself he was moving here to get away from entanglements and disturbances in his life. Trish and her sadness and who she was or wasn't living with weren't his problem.

His problem was a massive case of writer's block that was driving him crazy.

He moved through the house, liking it more and more. The immense kitchen had the feel of an old-fashioned great room, with a huge fireplace and a comfortable collection of mismatched overstuffed furniture that looked right in the room. It smelled like spices. Cinnamon, maybe?

Beyond the kitchen area a screened porch ran the length of the back of the house.

The room looked like the kind of place where a whole family might gather in the winter to eat and socialize. He recalled that the agent showing him the house had said parts of it dated to the eighteenth century.

He imagined in those days it would have been practical to confine daily activities to one room, given the limitations of heating and lighting.

He made a mental note to ask Joyce if the real estate agent had given her any history on the structure. If not, he'd do some research himself.

Fortunately the house now had modern electrical wiring, plumbing, central heat and updated appliances, but to him that didn't cut down on the appeal. Authenticity was great in theory but hell to live with.

Ian found the stairs and headed up to where he remembered the bedrooms were located. There was an airy upstairs corner room that would make a perfect office. The windows in the south wall overlooked an orchard, and from the windows in the east wall he could see the barn.

As soon as the animals were gone, he'd look into turning the barn into a proper garage.

He was pleased that he'd made the impulsive purchase. It was a perfect place to write. Quiet, private and secluded. He'd be able to settle down and finish his book.

He'd made it clear to Joyce the location of the farm was not to be divulged to anyone, not even his publisher. All communication would go through her.

The farm would be his haven from obsessive fans and shallow acquaintances who wanted his friendship for their own selfish reasons. He was unapologetic about being a recluse. His work required it, and his work came first.

He'd move the bed out and use the big worktable in the corner under the windows as a desk. The curtains would come down. There was no need for privacy way out here in the country.

He smiled as he considered the view again. From where he stood, the only house he could see was the old stone house beyond the barn.

Where Trish lived. The woman just popped into his head, uninvited.

He tried to concentrate on the house. He remembered the real estate agent telling him the tiny structure where the caretakers lived had been the original farmhouse on the property. It looked as if it couldn't be more than two rooms.

He wondered if she was comfortable in such a small space, then dismissed the thought. It was none of his business whether or not she was happy.

The only thing he needed to care about

in relation to her was that she did her job and stayed out of his way. From the look of the house, Ian had no complaints.

He glanced down at his watch. He needed to leave to get to his book signing on time, but he found he didn't want to go. He hated the ordeal, facing all those people who stood in line for hours just to have him scrawl his name inside the front cover.

They all wanted a personal conversation from him, some snippet they could carry away. Why? Why couldn't his book be enough?

The book he was working on now was so different from what he'd done before. His agent and his editor and Joyce had all subtly let him know they thought he was making a big mistake and he'd lose readers over it.

Maybe that was a good thing.

With a sigh he headed back down the stairs. The place was even more perfect than he remembered.

He couldn't wait to move in.

Chapter Three

Trish had Emma in a baby front pack, strapped to her chest. She'd buttoned them both up inside an oversize, heavy jacket. Only the top of the baby's head, covered with a pink knit cap, showed. Trish figured she probably looked like a bag lady, but Emma had a cold and she needed to be kept warm.

The horse dealer had just pulled up to the barn with a huge trailer. He jumped out of the cab of his truck and waved to her. "Ms. Ryan?" He pulled on gloves and opened the door of the trailer with a clang of metal.

"They're ready to go." She'd been in the barn with Max, saying goodbye.

It had been harder than she expected. She'd brought him apples and sugar, and he'd nudged her shoulder with his big head when she'd started to cry, as if he'd known what she was saying to him.

She chalked some of her emotion up to fatigue. Emma had a little fever and had been fussy and awake for a good part of the night. Trish had been up giving her baby sponge baths every hour.

"Okay, then. I have the paperwork here. I want to hurry before the storm hits." He pulled a sheaf of dog-eared papers from his back pocket.

Trish took the papers and looked to the north. It was only the middle of the morning, but the sky was almost black. She wondered how much time she had until the snow started.

There was still so much to do before Mr. Miller returned this weekend. She stood back as the horse dealer led the big gray into the trailer.

Trish went into the barn and took hold of Max's bridle, even though he'd probably follow her like a big old brown dog.

She got him out to the truck and the dealer held up his hand.

"I want him in last, 'cause he gets dropped off first."

Trish scratched Max under his chin. "I thought they were all going to the same auction."

"Not this guy. He's going to the slaughter-house. A lame old horse like him won't sell."

Trish felt as if she'd been hit in the belly with a fist. "You mean he's going to be put down?"

The man shrugged, his heavy sheepskin-lined jacket swallowing his ears for a moment. "Yup."

Her mind whirling she asked, "So you won't get any money for him?"

"Nah. But I won't charge your boss to drop him off."

Trish dropped Max's lead and shuffled through the papers the dealer had given her. Before she could talk herself out of it, she pulled out the sheet that belonged to Max. "So it doesn't matter if he stays?"

He shot her a surprised look. "Up to you. But a three-legged horse eats as much as one with four legs. Can't ride him, can you?"

Trish shook her head. She didn't ride any of them. That made no difference to her. Emma sneezed and Trish patted her through the heavy jacket.

She led Max back into his stall and closed the gate while the driver loaded the other two horses.

Why was she acting so crazy? Mr. Miller wanted all the animals gone. He'd been very clear on that point. She couldn't very well hide a horse. Or afford to feed him, she reminded herself.

She checked the feed bin. It was low, but with only Max eating, it would last for a while. She'd think of something.

She went out to the teamster's rig and signed the papers for the other animals in the trailer, then watched the driver pull away.

Calling herself a fool, she headed for the stone house. Maybe the people who lived out on the main road near the bus stop would let her pasture him there. They had young children and she could exchange his keep for baby-sitting. She'd check when she went for groceries.

She couldn't let Max be put down. He was too good a friend, and Trish had had so few loyal friends in her life.

She gathered up the laundry and the bag of Emma's dirty diapers and hauled it all up to the main house. She'd do her laundry tomorrow while she was cleaning.

She worked all day, stopping frequently to nurse Emma. Her little nose was so stuffed up she had a hard time eating.

Exhausted, Trish finally decided it was time to quit. With Emma bundled up in her arms, she opened the front door and was shocked to see two inches of snow had already fallen.

She locked the door and fought the wind, making a quick stop at the barn to feed and water Max, who stood dozing in his stall. Tollie, the mutt, had made a bed in a pile of hay outside Max's stall, and his tail thumped when she greeted him, his blind eyes staring right past her. Crew Cut, the cat with the scarred head and damaged ears, was curled up with the dog.

Tollie did pretty well, considering he couldn't see a thing, but she noticed he was staying in the barn more and more. She left the door open a crack so Tollie and Crew could get out if they needed to.

She let herself in the door of her house. It was almost as cold inside as it was out in the snow. She needed to get the fireplace going so the room would be warm enough for Emma.

They'd have to sleep in front of the fire again tonight. She flipped the switch of the lamp in the front room.

Nothing happened.

Trish groaned. The power was out already and the storm had just started. That meant no lights and no water, because the well pump was electric.

Still holding Emma, she turned around and headed back to the main house to get the generator going.

Trish unlocked the door and settled Emma, who was starting to fuss, on the couch with pillows around her to keep her from rolling off. Then she tackled the generator.

Within minutes she had the lights on and could hear the hum of the refrigerator. She could also hear the wind starting to howl around the house.

Trish turned on the television and listened to the news as she tried to nurse Emma again. The baby felt too warm and Trish tried to gauge her temperature. She was still running a little fever, which would account for her crankiness. Normally she was a very happy baby.

The local newscaster was predicting temperatures in the teens, high winds and two feet of snow.

There was no way Trish could keep Emma warm at the stone house. There was no heat besides the fireplace, and when the wind blew, the flue did not draw well and the air inside became smoky. With her stuffed-up nose Emma was having enough trouble breathing as it was.

She tucked the baby into the crook of her arm. "I guess we'll stay here tonight."

Emma smiled a toothless little lopsided grin, the first one Trish had seen all day.

"There's my girl. You like that idea?"

The baby gurgled and smiled again.

"We'll just camp out right here. I'll build

a fire and we can be nice and warm all night. We can even watch television."

Trish fixed herself a can of soup and made a mental note to replace it with her own money the next time she went to the grocery store. Just as she was finishing up she heard Tollie barking at the door to the screened porch on the side of the house.

She went out to let him in, and the chill took her breath away. The dog was caked with snow, and she had to shove against the screen door to close it, because of the wind. Just before she got it shut, Crew squeezed through the small opening and ran through the main door and into the house.

She brushed the old dog off before letting him in, then put a frayed towel in the corner near a heater vent and led him to the spot.

"If you're staying in, you'll stay there."

Tollie turned around three times and then plopped down on the towel, apparently pleased with the arrangement. She could just see Crew's tail under the china cabinet.

Trish lit the fire in the huge stone fireplace, then got out blankets from the linen closet and settled Emma and herself for the night, sinking into the soft cushions of the couch and savoring the luxury of sleeping in a warm room.

Exhausted, she didn't even turn on the television and drifted off to sleep almost immediately, the sound of the storm howling around the house strangely soothing.

Tollie's furious barking woke her up. Groggily she raised her head and looked around the dark room, wondering what had set the mutt off. Then she realized she wasn't at home, she was at the main house.

She had no idea how long she'd been asleep, and the red glowing numbers of the digital clock on the microwave flashed 12:00. She hadn't reset it after turning the generator on.

Just as she was about to get up and investigate what might be upsetting her normally placid dog, the overhead lights went on, blinding her.

She peered over the back of the couch, squinting into the bright light. To her horror, Ian Miller stood in the doorway to the great room. The shoulders of his coat were thick with snow, and there was a thunderous expression on his face.

He took his gaze off her for just a moment to glance over at Tollie, who stood stiff-legged and growling, all the hair

41

raised on his back.

"What are you doing here?" she blurted out without thinking. He wasn't due for two more days.

He set his bag down with a thud. "I might ask you the same question," he fairly growled at her.

Trish felt her heart sink. He'd fire her. Probably tonight, considering the furious expression on his face.

She told Tollie to hush and wondered where she could go. What was she going to do? She had no money, no marketable skills and no family. She still owed the hospital and the funeral home. She'd been homeless before, and she wasn't going to let her baby live that kind of life. Ever. She looked down at her sleeping daughter, overwhelmed with dismay.

Ian stared at the tousled, delightful-looking woman curled up on his couch, her big blue eyes blinking against the light. He felt like Papa Bear come home to find Goldilocks in his bed.

Except he didn't think Goldilocks had had a demented-looking mutt. At her command the dog had downgraded his barking to growls, and his spooky white eyes were staring past Ian. Ian watched Trish, but

42

didn't take his full attention off the dog.

She appeared to be confused and scared and still managed to look utterly enchanting.

Just what he needed, he thought, rubbing the tense muscles in the back of his neck. His dream of utter solitude dissolved in annoyance.

He was exhausted from fighting the storm all the way from Philadelphia. He'd decided this afternoon when he'd heard the weather predictions that if he waited to leave he'd be forced to delay the trip, possibly for days, and he couldn't stand the thought of being stranded in the city when he could be at Blacksmith Farm. So he'd decided to come early.

He should have called to warn her, but it hadn't occurred to him she'd be in his house.

"Well?" He was still waiting for her explanation.

She swallowed hard and made a helpless little gesture with her hand. "The power went out. No lights or water."

He glanced up at the ceiling fixture. Did she think he was an idiot? "Looks like it came back."

She shook her head full of tousled, blond curls. "This house is on a generator."

"No generator at the stone house?"

She shook her head again and continued to stare at him as if he were Attila the Hun.

Just then a cat that looked as though it had gotten its head and tail caught in a piece of farm equipment sauntered into the room and jumped up onto the arm of the couch. Absently she scratched it under the chin, and Ian could hear the rumbling of its purr all the way across the room.

He looked around, wondering how many other animals might be lurking in the corners. At least the dog had settled down. The sound of her voice caught his attention.

"Mr. Miller?" She put the cat aside, struggled out of her nest of blankets and stood up. She was wearing pink flannel pajamas printed with yellow rubber ducks.

She looked as though she might cry. "I'm sorry to be here," she said, her voice hitching, "but the baby has a cold and I needed to keep her warm."

Baby? What baby? Ian looked around the room again, wondering how he had managed to stumble into this weird nightmare. "Baby?"

She pointed to a wash basket beside the couch. Ian took a step forward and saw a miniature version of Trish asleep in the basket.

He was hit with a punch of emotions that left him speechless and angry. He didn't want the confused feelings that welled up and took him completely by surprise. She had a baby. This woman who looked like a child herself was a mother.

She started folding up the blankets with jerky movements. "I'm really sorry about this, Mr. Miller. I'll get dressed and go home."

She obviously hadn't looked outside recently. They were in the beginning of a whiteout.

"No," he said sharply, appalled at the idea. She couldn't take a baby, sick or otherwise, out in this weather, not to mention live without power.

She probably wouldn't even be able to find the stone house, even though it was only a short distance away.

She stopped folding the blankets and stared at him, her chin trembling. "No?"

Feeling uncharacteristically protective, he said, "Absolutely not." He wasn't going to let her take a step outside. She was such a little thing the drifts would come up to her waist.

She began blinking rapidly, as if she had something in her eye. "But where am I supposed to go?"

He wondered how sharp a brain she had under all those blond curls. Usually he didn't have so much trouble communicating, but for some reason she didn't seem to understand. Annoyed, he said, "Nowhere. You'll stay here."

He told himself he didn't care if she was unhappy, but the misery on her face made him want to take her in his arms. Oh, yes, he definitely needed to get her back to the stone house as soon as possible. He'd order a second generator in the morning.

"Oh." She sat back down on the couch, hugging the half-folded blanket to her chest. "Thank you."

Ian glanced out the window. "Where is the baby's father?" His voice sounded gruffer than he had intended. It was none of his business, but he needed to know, and that irritated him.

She swallowed hard and got a very strange look on her face. After a long pause she said, "Not here."

Odd answer, he thought. The father should be the one worrying about her and their child, not him. He didn't want the entanglement. "I have my cell phone. Can you call him?"

She blinked several more times. "Uh, no, probably not."

What kind of answer was that? Either she could or she couldn't. What did she mean, *probably* not?

She was acting very strangely. He studied her for a long moment, trying to read her odd behavior. "Trish, *where* is the baby's father?"

She swallowed hard several times and stared at the floor. Then she raised her chin and looked right at him with those big, blue eyes. "He's dead."

Completely taken aback, Ian could only stare at her. Finally he said, "Dead?"

She nodded, her eyes welling with tears.

He didn't know what to say. No wonder she looked so upset.

Now he really felt like he was in the middle of a bizarre nightmare. He wanted to know when and how the man had died, but because she looked so scared and hurt, he couldn't bring himself to ask.

She must have loved him very much. Ian didn't have the faintest idea why that should bother him.

Chapter Four

Trish couldn't look at Mr. Miller. She stared into the fire, sure that when he got over the shock of hearing about Billy's death he'd come to his senses and fire her.

She was so lost in her misery that when he spoke she jumped. She hadn't heard him walk up beside her.

"Do you need any help with the arrangements?"

Her mind went blank. Arrangements? What was he talking about?

He waited patiently for a moment. "The funeral. Do you need me to call anyone for you?"

Of course. He thought Billy had just died. He didn't know she'd been widowed for two and a half months — because she'd been afraid of losing her job so she'd covered it up.

His kindness nearly undid her. She shook her head. "No. It's all over."

She hadn't been able to afford a funeral. There really hadn't been anyone to attend, anyway. She'd asked Billy's best friend to get his ashes from the funeral home because she didn't have a car to go and pick them up.

A few days later he'd called to tell her Billy's drinking buddies had had a memorial service for him down at the Stumble Inn, their favorite establishment. Apparently, it didn't occur to them to ask her to come. She'd never asked him what he'd done with the ashes.

"When did he die?"

She would have to tell him, then he'd know she'd been lying to him all along. "Two and a half months ago." She looked up into his startled face.

"I see." He picked up his bag and, without another word, turned and left the room.

She watched him go, then choked back tears as she looked down at her sleeping daughter and whispered, "I'm sorry, sweetheart." She could actually feel her security slip away.

She had been foolish to think she'd be able to deceive everyone and keep both their jobs so she'd have the old stone house. Swallowing a sob, she stared miserably into the fire. What was she going to do?

Trish hated feeling sorry for herself.

She'd learned a long time ago it was a waste of time and got you nothing.

Knock it off, she told herself fiercely. He hadn't actually said he was going to fire her, and she *had* been taking care of things since Billy died.

Heck, she'd taken care of things since she'd discovered she was pregnant and moved in with Billy.

He'd usually been hung over in the mornings and stayed in bed, then he would take off in the afternoon to drink beer with his buddies or fish or go hunting.

Trish decided to go and talk to Mr. Miller and present her case before he had too much time to think about what he had just learned. She had to convince him to keep her on. She'd proven she could do the job, hadn't she?

She tucked the blanket around Emma and then raced into the utility room behind the kitchen. She couldn't go talk to him in pajamas with ducks all over them. She pulled her laundry out of the dryer, yanked off her pajamas and scrambled into a pair of jeans and a flannel shirt.

She checked on Emma again, banked the fire and then headed up the stairs to the bedrooms. She paused at the first door with the light on. There was a black case

50

on the big worktable under the window, and his wet overcoat was draped over the chair, dripping water all over the floor, but no Mr. Miller.

She continued on down the hall to the next room and stopped dead in the doorway. He was standing at the closet with his back to her.

His bare back.

Her eyes lingered on the smooth expanse of skin covering his broad shoulders and tapering down to a trim waist.

Trish felt her mouth go dry. The man was built like a Greek god. Who knew that much male perfection lay under his beautiful clothes?

She must have made a noise because he glanced over his shoulder at her before she could back away.

"Do you need something, Ms. Ryan?" he asked, sounding thoroughly annoyed, his words muffled as he pulled a sweater over his head.

She could feel the color burn in her cheeks. He turned and watched her as she tried to remember why she had charged up the stairs.

She'd been too impulsive and hadn't given herself time to think about what she was going to say. Maybe this wasn't the

51

best time to bring up her future employment. She needed to be really sure he was in a good mood before she broached the subject.

Desperately she searched for a reason to be standing in the door to his bedroom. "I was, ah, wondering if you needed, that is, if you wanted anything to eat?"

Absently he rubbed his hand over his flat stomach, now covered by a soft sweater that brought out the incredible blue of his eyes. "Can you make me a sandwich?"

Trish brightened. She knew her way around the kitchen. A full stomach would put him in a good mood. "Of course. Ham? Turkey?"

She had shopped yesterday when a neighbor had offered her a ride to the market. Gratefully she had accepted. It was so much easier than dragging Emma and the groceries on the bus, so she had stocked up.

He seemed to carefully consider his choice. "Ham. With everything on it. And coffee if you have it."

She nodded and turned to leave. "Ms. Ryan?"

"Yes?" She had to brace herself not to flinch as he studied her. She couldn't read his face. Was he going to give her notice before she could even make him supper?

"I'll eat up here. I'm going to use that first room as an office after I move some of the stuff out of it. Would you bring the sandwich up here?"

"Sure." Trish exhaled a long breath as she turned to leave his bedroom.

"And, Ms. Ryan?"

She swung back to face him. "Yes?"

"When I'm working, do not disturb me, for any reason. Understood?"

She nodded. How could anyone not understand that tone of voice? "I understand."

She left quickly and stopped by the first bedroom and grabbed his coat to take it downstairs so she could hang it to dry, and reminded herself to bring a rag up to mop the water on the floor when she brought up his sandwich.

When she returned with his sandwich and an insulated pot of coffee, he was already at work on a laptop computer, his long, strong-looking fingers flying over the keys. She set the tray down at his elbow, and he mumbled something without looking up.

She mopped up the floor and left the room quickly, not wanting to disturb his work. If anything would get her fired, she guessed it was that.

She decided not to change into her pajamas in case he needed anything else. She lay down on the couch and tried to doze, but found herself wide awake, trying to come up with what she was going to say to Ian Miller to convince him to keep her on as the caretaker for Blacksmith Farm.

Emma began to stir and Trish scooped her up before she could cry.

She nuzzled the sleepy baby's sweet-smelling neck and cooed, "Hungry, pretty girl?" Emma gurgled a reply and, one-handed, Trish deftly undid the buttons on her flannel shirt, then settled into the corner of the couch and nursed her baby.

Trish whispered down at her daughter, "Don't worry. We'll convince him we can do this job." She picked up the mystery she'd been reading and read aloud to Emma as she nursed.

Trish hoped she was right about being able to win over her new boss, because she had no idea what she would do if Mr. Miller decided to get a new caretaker.

Trish finished feeding Emma, changed her diaper and settled her back in the basket. She lay down on the couch, physically exhausted, but with her mind churning, unable to sleep.

Finally she got up and prowled through the downstairs looking for something to do. She'd already cleaned the house from top to bottom. She plumped the cushions on the couch in the front room and straightened the rag rugs, then headed back to the kitchen.

She could get a head start on dinner for tomorrow night. Cooking always gave her time to think. Maybe she could come up with a plan while she put together the ingredients for a stew.

She gathered up what she needed from the refrigerator and began peeling and chopping and browning. The rhythm of the work made her relax.

"What the hell are you doing?"

She jumped at the sound of his voice behind her.

He was standing there with the coffeepot in his hand, a thunderous expression on his face.

She just couldn't seem to do anything right tonight. "I'm making dinner."

He looked at her as if she'd lost her mind. "It's 2:00 a.m."

"For tomorrow night." She glanced at the clock. "Well, I guess since it's after midnight it would be for tonight." Great, now she was babbling.

His scowl got fiercer. "You look exhausted. Why are you cooking in the middle of the night?"

"I couldn't sleep." She wanted to ask him why he was up, but bit back the question. He didn't look tired. He looked wonderful. His hair was a little mussed, as if he'd run his fingers through it, but it just made him look even more appealing.

He thrust the coffeepot at her. "Well, stop."

She took it from him, then turned and surveyed the kitchen.

Pots and pans filled the big sink. She was halfway through the preparation of two more dinners. She looked at the mess on the counter and the casserole dishes lined up. She had intended just to put together the stew, but then things had gotten away from her.

There was at least an hour of work left. She didn't want to stop now.

"I'll make you more coffee," she said cautiously, hoping he'd go back upstairs so she could finish. Maybe he only wrote at night. She'd read that some writers did that.

"I can make my own coffee," he said gruffly and reached to take the pot back, his hands covering hers.

Trish stood still for a moment as the warmth of his palms caressed the backs of her hands. She pulled away, trying to ignore the pleasurable sensation the slide of his smooth, warm palms caused over her chapped, reddened skin.

Taking a deep breath to calm her fluttering pulse, she turned and put the jug down on the counter. "I'll do it," she said, still facing away from him.

She turned and looked over her shoulder at him. "I just have to put this stuff back in the refrigerator before I go to bed. I'll bring the coffee up to you."

"I will not tolerate any interruption of my work," he said, repeating his earlier admonition. He stared at her for a moment, then turned abruptly and left the room.

From the way she saw things, *he* had interrupted *her*. Annoyed, she filled the coffeemaker with fresh ground coffee and water, then raced to tidy up the counter as the fragrant brew dripped into the pot.

The last thing she needed to do was make him angry, although she couldn't figure out why her cooking in the middle of the night would be a problem for him. He wasn't paying her by the hour.

She poured the coffee into the insulated pot, wrapped a handful of store-bought cookies in a napkin and took everything up to him.

He sat hunched over the laptop computer, his broad shoulders blocking the screen. He didn't look up when she set the coffee and cookies on a corner of the huge worktable he was using as a desk.

Trish tiptoed downstairs and finished up what she was doing and got ready for bed. She nursed Emma and settled her back in her basket, then she lay on the couch for a long time, trying to get to sleep without visions of Ian Miller crowding into her thoughts.

Ian stood at the window of his office, moodily looking over the roof of the barn to the old stone farmhouse. He'd spent the morning moving some of the room's furniture out, including an old iron crib he'd disassembled. For now everything was stored in the small bedroom at the end of the hall.

He glanced around. The room suited him very well as an office. He hoped he'd be able to keep getting work done, but he wasn't optimistic. All the pages he'd churned out last night were probably just a lucky break.

He was stuck with the housekeeper

sharing the house until the blizzard stopped. Her presence was always in the back of his mind, and he kept wondering what she was doing, even when he couldn't hear her or see her.

She was such a jumpy little thing, acting as if he was some kind of ogre, and it annoyed him.

The creative streak he'd had last night had been a fluke. It must have been. He'd never been able to write when someone else was around. He turned his attention back to the scene outside.

His car was completely covered. According to the morning news, the blizzard had dumped three feet of snow, but in some places the drifts were up to the eaves.

If he didn't remember where he'd parked, he would never know his car was there. In fact, the scene looked the way it must have two hundred years ago when the stone farmhouse had been built. There was nothing he could see that could be identified as twenty-first century. The pristine quality of the countryside had a magical look to it.

The meteorologist on the local weather channel had announced there was another storm coming in behind this one. They could expect more snow tonight.

He wished the inside of his house was as quiet and peaceful as the landscape. He'd bought the farm as a retreat, to be alone so he could write. He had anticipated having the house all to himself. Now he was sharing it with a woman, a baby, a cat and a dog.

What had surprised him more than anything was he *had* been able to write last night. In spite of the chaos inside the house he'd written two chapters that pleased him. He was *never* pleased with a first draft.

The book he was working on was important to him, more important than any of his best-sellers. It was the book he had always wanted to write. The book his agent and publisher had steered him away from. They kept telling him it wasn't what his fans wanted, what they expected. Ian thought his fans would understand. And if they didn't, he thought sourly, they could skip buying it.

He suspected that was the reason everyone was having a problem with this project. His agent and editor were afraid it wouldn't sell well and make the big money his other books had.

He didn't care what they thought. The time was right for him to write this story, and he was going to finish the book. He would like to blame his writer's block on them, but he couldn't. He wanted so much to do a good job on this book he was pretty sure *he* was the one standing in his own way.

He forced his thoughts away from the book and back to the practical. He needed to make sure they had enough gasoline for the generator so they could stay warm. From the looks of the refrigerator, they didn't need to worry about food for a month. His housekeeper cooked like a madwoman.

And what was he going to do about her? She couldn't continue to do all the work around this place. It was too much for one person, especially a slender little thing like her. He wondered how old she was. She looked about seventeen.

How long had she been married? How had her husband died? There were so many questions he wanted to ask. The need for answers surprised him. He never wanted to get involved in other people's private lives.

He'd have Joyce tell the property manager to find someone to help around the farm with the grounds. Trish could still do the housekeeping and live in the stone farmhouse. The caretaker would have to be a day job.

He bent down to jot a note to himself to ask Joyce to look into it the next time he talked to her. Then he wrote a note to himself. "Ignore the housekeeper. She's none of your business."

He straightened up and scowled at his own handwriting.

He crumpled the piece of paper and tossed it in the trash. Since when did he need to remind himself of something like that?

Chapter Five

A scraping noise drew Ian out of his manuscript. Annoyed at the interruption, he glanced at the computer and was amazed to find he was well into the middle third of the draft.

He hadn't had a creative streak like this for months. He'd been sure he wouldn't be able to write until his housekeeper moved back to her house, but he'd been wrong.

He stood and stretched, then looked at the time display in the upper corner of the screen to discover it was well past lunchtime.

No wonder his stomach was growling for food. He'd been working since early this morning on nothing but coffee.

He opened his office door and found out where the scraping noise was coming from. Trish was on the landing on her hands and knees, totally absorbed in hand sanding the floor. Her blond curls bounced as she ran the block wrapped with sandpaper over the boards.

He could see how red and chapped her

hands were from where he stood. "What the hell are you doing?"

She jumped at the sound of his voice. Her head jerked up, and a look of panic crossed her face, then was gone as quickly as it had appeared.

She scrambled to her feet. "Is it bothering you? I don't have to do this now," she said in a rush of words.

She was wearing another of those ratty flannel shirts. He wondered how many she had, then chided himself. His housekeeper's wardrobe was none of his business.

"I'm hungry." He rubbed his hand over his growling stomach.

She looked relieved at his statement. "I made soup. And sandwiches. Is that okay?"

"Fine." Now that she mentioned it, he could smell the soup. He started down the steps, then stopped. "Is it okay to walk on these?"

She nodded and her curls bounced. "Oh, yes. I'm going to do a half at a time, so you can still use the stairs." She spoke quickly and gestured nervously to the steps.

He looked down at the steps. "What exactly are you doing?"

With a shrug she said, "They were getting scratched, so I'm refinishing them."

Refinishing? They looked fine to him, but she seemed so nervous he wasn't going to mention it.

He followed her down the steps. She stopped at the bottom to pick up a wastebasket covered by a thin towel.

He watched her balance the basket carefully in her two hands. "Is the baby in there?"

Her expression softened. "Yes. She's sleeping. I put the towel over her to keep the dust off while I sanded."

"Do you ever let her out?" He was amused by the way she carted the baby around like a load of laundry.

Her back stiffened, and she got an insulted expression on her face. "Of course. She's asleep now."

Did she think he was questioning her mothering techniques? He was just curious and knew nothing about babies. He groped around for something to say. "Does she crawl yet?"

Trish set the basket down on the counter in the kitchen and folded the towel back. "She's just three months old. Babies don't usually start to crawl until they're around seven or eight months old." Her voice changed when she spoke about her daughter.

"I see. What are you going to do when she can climb out of that basket?"

Again the look of alarm flashed across her face. "I'll get a playpen. I'll be able to get all my work done," she said quickly.

She was the touchiest woman Ian had ever met. No matter what he said she seemed to react badly.

She turned to the stove and got busy serving up a bowl of soup. He took a seat at the table, flipped on the television to a news channel and watched her quick movements as she worked around the kitchen. He hadn't been questioning her efficiency. If anything, she worked too hard.

His mind drifted back to his manuscript as she set his food in front of him. He needed another character in the book. Someone with a past, who could reveal secrets about the protagonist.

As he ate he watched Trish out of the corner of his eye. His thoughts drifted through the possibilities of the new character. Maybe she would look like Trish.

As his ideas about the new character jelled and took form, he went upstairs and back to his work.

Ian worked through the afternoon and finally ran out of steam. He stood to stretch and saw a small figure in a bright red knit cap and oversize jacket emerge from under the eaves of the porch. It had to be Trish, but it was impossible to tell who was inside the bundle of clothes. He watched as she struggled through the waist deep snow toward the barn. What the hell did she think she was doing?

He bounded down the stairs and through the great room. The laundry basket that her baby slept in was in front of the couch. The blind dog lay beside the basket, along with a white plastic thing with an antenna that looked like a small radio.

When he leaned over the basket to glance at the sleeping baby, the dog growled low in his throat and stared at a space beside Ian.

Ian left the sleeping child to her canine protector and headed through the kitchen. He'd not yet been in this part of the house, but there must be an outside door because she had emerged from this area.

He went through a utility room, warm from the heat being put off by the dryer, past a bedroom and then came to a mudroom.

His overcoat was hanging there, as well as a couple of old jackets. He grabbed one that looked as if it would fit, pulled ratty old leather gloves out of one of the pockets and yanked them onto his hands. He pulled a wool scarf off another hook along with a knit cap, put them on. He removed his shoes and stepped into a pair of lined rubber barn boots that were at least a size too small.

Ready to face the elements, he yanked open the back door.

The cold air hit him like a slap in the face. It must be twenty below. Why would she have risked these conditions to go to the barn? The only possibility he could come up with was she had parked her car in the barn and needed something she had left inside.

He followed her trail in the snow, struggling through the deep white powder. How had she managed to plow through this?

He didn't care why she was out here, he told himself. He wasn't worried about her, only curious. Besides, he had his own reasons for going to the barn. It would give him a chance to look around and see how much work needed to be done to turn it into a proper garage. He would dig his car out sooner or later, and it would be good to have a place to store it out of the elements.

He stopped to catch his breath, the cold air burning his lungs even as he breathed through the wool scarf. Actually, if he was going to live here at the farm, it might be a good idea to get a truck. One with four-wheel drive. The driveway up to the house wasn't paved, and in bad weather would be impassable in his sports car.

He made it to the big sliding barn door and slipped through the opening. He stood for a moment and let his eyes adjust to the dim light. There was a large open space inside the door with plenty of room to park several vehicles, but it was empty. So much for his theory about her retrieving something from her car.

Beyond the open space there was a wide center aisle with stalls on each side. It smelled of hay and dust and animals.

He heard Trish talking in a low voice, but he couldn't make out the words.

Was someone out here? Someone she had come to meet? The thought made him angry. Not, he told himself quickly as he strained to hear what she was saying, because she was meeting someone. This was his place. He deserved to know if someone was hiding in the barn.

He strode down the long center aisle to investigate, then came to an abrupt stop when he spotted her.

She was backing out of a stall, still murmuring to whoever was in there. The jacket she wore hung to her knees, and she'd rolled the sleeves up until they formed huge doughnuts of fabric around her slender wrists.

She must have sensed he was there because her head jerked up and she spun around to face him. Her face held a comical mix of guilt, surprise and dismay.

He watched the expressions on her face as he waited for her to say something.

Just then an enormous horse followed her out of the stall. The horse dipped his head and playfully butted her in the middle of her back, propelling her toward him. She let out a little shriek of surprise and stumbled. He took a step forward and caught her up under her arms, hauling her back to her feet. She couldn't weigh more than a hundred pounds.

He let go of her, uneasy that he was so relieved she had come out into the deep snow for a horse and not a man.

She jerked away from him and turned back to the horse. Ian would swear the horse looked amused. He looked as if he was smiling. Ian could see big yellow teeth under his horsey lips as he snorted and shook his giant head.

"Max!" She grasped his halter in both hands and pushed. "You bad boy. Get back in your stall."

Ian knew nothing about horses. He held his breath and wondered if it was a good idea for her to get so close to an animal who was ten times bigger than she was. Seemingly unconcerned, she pushed at him as if he was a placid dog.

She didn't seem to notice that the beast's hoofs were very close to smashing her toes as she shoved him backward.

When she had pushed him back in his stall, he neatly plucked the knit cap off her head with his teeth and dropped it on the ground at her feet.

Ian started to breathe again as she closed the half door, shutting the horse in. She stooped over to pick up the cap, stepped out of range of the horse and whacked the hat against her leg to dislodge the bits of hay that stuck to it.

Finally she looked up at Ian with a guilty expression and gestured toward the stall. "It's a horse."

She jammed the old red hat back over her head.

Ian struggled not to smile. "I figured that out. Who does he belong to?" All the stock that had come with the farm was supposed to have been sold.

Her stubborn chin came up in a defiant jut. "He's mine now." Then her expression changed and she seemed to battle with herself, more emotions flitting across her cute little face.

The thought occurred to Ian that this woman should never play poker. Her face was so expressive she'd never be able to bluff a hand.

"Well, technically, he's yours." She curled her hands into fists. "But I couldn't let him go to the knacker. So I kept him."

She stood on the balls of her feet like a bantam-weight boxer. She didn't even come up to his shoulder and she looked ready to take him on.

Ian looked at the grizzled chin of the big brown horse and then back at her. "The dealer couldn't sell him?"

"No. He's old and lame." She blinked and chewed her lip again. "I'll pay you for him."

She looked like a miniature bag lady in her oversize raggedy jacket and boots. She had a baby, a dog and a cat already. He didn't know how much he paid her to be his housekeeper beyond her room and board, but he guessed it wasn't much. The last thing she looked like she needed was a lame horse. An animal that size had to be expensive to maintain.

"Why? Why do you want him? An old three-legged horse must not be good for much."

She shrugged, and her eyes filled with tears. Blinking rapidly, she turned away from him and headed toward the door without answering his question.

He felt a touch of panic at her sudden emotion. What was he going to do if she started to cry? He wasn't comfortable with emotion. Women he knew wouldn't shed tears over a mangy animal.

To his relief she seemed to pull herself together as she drew what looked like a white walkie-talkie out of her pocket. "I have to get back to the house. Emma will be waking up soon."

Obviously he'd touched a nerve. He certainly had no intention of prying into her life, but it was his farm, and he didn't want the complications of animals.

Intrigued by her defense of the animal, he let the subject of the horse drop and fell into step behind her. There was plenty of time to discuss the horse. He didn't want it there, but if the alternative was having it put down, he wondered if he could make that decision.

He suspected she didn't have any other place to keep it for now. "I'm going to turn the barn into a garage."

She kept walking toward the door with her head down. "You need the whole barn? How many cars do you own?"

"Just one. But I may get something with four-wheel drive for the country."

He thought he heard her snort softly, but he couldn't be sure. Then he remembered thinking her car would be in the barn. "Where do you keep your car?"

She glanced up at him. "I don't have a car. It was totaled in the accident," she said rather matter-of-factly.

He didn't remember her mentioning an accident, then he remembered that her husband had died recently. "The accident that killed your husband?"

She nodded. It didn't escape him that she had gotten more emotional talking about the horse than her husband, but there was no way he was going to broach that topic, so he changed the subject. "What's that in your hand?"

She held up the plastic device. "A baby monitor."

That explained the thing by the baby's basket. Before he could ask her how it worked, she slipped through the opening in the barn door.

He followed her and closed the door behind him.

He walked behind her as she struggled through the deep snow. She certainly was a determined little thing.

His retreat was nothing like he'd imagined.

Oh well, he thought as he resisted catching up to her to help her, as soon as the electricity was on again she'd be returning to the stone house with her baby and her menagerie.

The important thing was his life was back on track. He had found the twist he needed for the book. The new character he'd created was going to work, and at the rate he was going, the first draft would be finished in record time.

Living at the farm was better than he'd imagined. The problem with the horse could be handled later.

He wasn't so sure his growing feelings for Trish would be as easy to deal with.

Chapter Six

After three days, the power was back on in the area. Ian decided he needed to get Trish and her baby moved back to the farmhouse. She was too much of a distraction. He was getting a tremendous amount of writing done, more than he had expected, but he was constantly aware that she was, well, *there*.

He didn't want to investigate the situation too much, but it was getting worse as time went by, and he needed it to stop.

He didn't have time in his life for her or her baby and the sooner she was not living under the same roof the better.

He went downstairs and found her curled up on the couch, sound asleep, the baby tucked protectively into the curve of her body. It was no wonder she needed a nap. She worked nonstop all day while the baby slept, and he'd heard her up in the night several times. She seemed to have the bad luck to have a nocturnal child.

Unsettled by his thoughts of her, he stood staring down at the two of them for a few moments, then roused himself. This was *exactly* the reason he needed them living elsewhere.

They were a distraction.

He didn't allow distractions in his life.

Quietly he made his way to the mudroom and shrugged into his heavy jacket. He strapped on a pair of snowshoes he found hanging by the door, picked up a snow shovel and set out across the yard.

He'd ask Joyce to send his cross-country skis. He loved to ski cross country and this was certainly a great place to do it. He wondered if Trish skied, then was surprised the thought had occurred to him. One of the things he loved about cross-country skiing was the solitude.

He stopped in at the barn and hunted around until he found a bin of feed for the horse. He approached Max gingerly, not at all confident of the horse's welcome. His lack of expertise annoyed him. This wasn't his job, but he didn't want Trish trudging through the snow, either.

He stood staring at the big animal. He'd never owned a pet in his life and now his household included a cat and a dog and a horse.

Three strays, he thought. A blind dog, a scarred cat and a lame horse. Coincidence? He didn't believe in it. Why did she pick up all these cast-off animals?

Ian left the barn and continued on to the stone farmhouse. He hadn't realized how small the place was. All he could see from his office was the roof.

He dug around the door until he could get it open, then drove the shovel into the snow and let himself into the house.

He started to remove his jacket, then realized it was as cold inside as it was out. He stood on the small frayed rug just inside the door and looked around in disbelief. The entire place was only two small rooms. Actually one big room divided in two.

The half of the room he stood in looked like a combination kitchen and living room, dominated by a big fireplace made of the same gray stone as the house. There was a shabby couch in front of the fireplace and a bassinet. A stack of folded blankets took up one end of the couch.

The only lighting was a yellowed plastic ceiling fixture consisting of one bulb. The wiring, patched in places with tape, ran along the ceiling and down the wall to a plug, and wiring for that had been pulled in through a small hole drilled in the stone wall. A small, rusty space heater was also plugged into the outlet. He looked around and realized it was the only electrical outlet in the room.

Someone had built a counter along a back wall that served as the kitchen. There were several open shelves that held a few pots and pans, dishes and canned goods, and a small, chipped propane stove that looked as if it had been installed in the twenties, along with a stained porcelain sink.

A single water pipe came into the house through the wall, just like the wiring. There was a tiny propane refrigerator that completed the kitchen.

The back portion of the house had been walled off with flimsy wood paneling. He crossed the room and looked in the door. The walled-off area formed a very small bedroom dominated by an old, iron double bed. Hooks held a few clothes in the bedroom and there was a small dresser. No closet. A similar lighting fixture with external wiring graced the bedroom.

A tiny bathroom, with fixtures that had to be eighty years old, was crowded into a corner.

Everything in the house was old, worn and shabby, but painfully neat and tidy.

Ian walked back to the front room. This was the twenty-first century. How could Trish live like this?

Then the thought hit him. This wasn't

Trish's house. She lived here, but it belonged to him. She probably didn't even own the furniture. That made him a slum landlord in the worst sense of the word.

An unreasonable sense of shame fueled his anger. He should have checked this out when he bought the property, but it hadn't crossed his mind. He'd been too busy making sure his own needs would be met.

He stomped out the front door, slamming it behind him. What the hell was he going to do now?

There was no way he could send her back here to live until he did extensive renovations on the place. He wondered if it would be possible to make enough improvements to upgrade the house to a livable condition.

Hell, maybe he should tear out the wiring and the other ancient upgrades and return it to its original condition. He could have it declared a historic landmark, he thought sourly. How many homes like this were left in America?

He plowed his way through the snow, headed for the warmth and comfort of the plank house, his mind working furiously on the problem of where Trish was going to live.

The farm was so far out that if she lived

in town she'd have a long commute. Then there was the difficulty of her not having a car.

Irked at the disruption in his day, he attempted to put his thoughts in order. He didn't want her in town. He wanted her here, where he wouldn't have to worry about her.

Ian abruptly stopped walking. Why would he even have a thought like that? She was the housekeeper. He liked the way she took care of things and wanted her available, that was all. There was no need to complicate the situation.

Still annoyed, he resumed his trek toward the porch.

A few days ago he would never have considered the option of her staying in the house with him, but now he knew he could write with her here.

Maybe he could get used to the idea.

Then another thought occurred to him. She might not want to continue to stay in the house. For some reason he seemed to make her nervous, and that annoyed him, too.

He was spending far too much time thinking about Trish.

He slipped off the snowshoes and stomped the caked snow off his boots.

Nervous or not, he decided, if she wanted the job, she'd have to stay.

Trish heard him out on the porch and realized he'd walked right past her while she slept on the couch.

Stupid, she thought. What would he think of her, sleeping in the middle of the day? She hurried over to the stove and stirred the thick tomato sauce simmering for dinner.

Aware of the moment Ian came through the door, she could feel him looking at her.

Trish plastered a forced smile on her face and turned around. His face was ruddy from the cold, his jaw shadowed by two days of beard.

She swallowed a sigh. He looked as good in his rough state as he did freshly shaved, wearing cashmere. Nature had given him more than a fair share of her bounty.

"Did you have a nice walk?" she asked brightly.

He just stared at her, a muscle jumping in his clenched jaw. "Well, it was bracing," he said, his tone tense.

She stiffened at the edge in his voice.

"I stopped by the barn and made sure the horse had food and water."

He was angry about Max. Trish wiped

her damp hands on her apron, then turned to the stove and began to furiously stir the sauce again. She was going to have to find a place for the horse.

"Oh," she said, trying to keep her voice steady. "You didn't need to bother with that. I was going to do it this afternoon."

He'd made it abundantly clear he'd wanted the animals cleared off. She chided herself for not making the arrangements before now.

He ignored her comment. "After I stopped by the barn I went down to the stone house to see if everything was okay."

She stood very still, the cooking spoon suspended over the pot. He was in her home? She knew he owned the house, but it was her *home*. Slowly she half turned to face him.

He stared at her for another long moment, then ran his big square hand through his hair. "You can't live there."

She dropped the spoon into the sauce and was only vaguely aware that the splatter burned her hand. She made two tries before she could get her voice to work. "Why not?"

He was talking about her *home*. A feeling of panic bloomed in her chest. "What's happened?"

He looked angry at her question. "Nothing's happened. That's the problem." He shoved his hands into his pockets, then drew them out and gestured in the general direction of the stone house. "Nothing has been done to the place for what, eighty years?"

She didn't know what to say. Was he angry that she hadn't made improvements?

"You can't live there until I get someone in to renovate it."

Renovate? What did he mean? It would take time to do that. Where was she going to live in the meantime?

She wiped her hands on her apron and took a deep breath. He was upset, and she didn't want him to make any hasty decisions.

"It's fine, really," she said in a rush. "You don't need to do that. Emma and I are happy there, really."

"Trish, there's nothing 'fine' about it. The place is a fire trap with that wiring. And there isn't adequate heat. No hot water. The stove and refrigerator belong in a museum. Should I go on?"

Miserable, Trish shook her head. He was right, but everything worked. She was very careful with the propane gas and electricity. She opened her mouth to tell him that, and he cut her off.

"It isn't a good place to keep a baby."

No, she had to admit, but it was better than homeless shelters and a couple of the foster homes she'd been in. It was clean. But he'd never been in a shelter or he'd realize how wonderful the stone house was, how safe she felt there.

"But really, I'm used to it and —"

He cut her off with a grim look. "Trish, staying at the stone house in its current condition is not an option. Period."

"Oh." From the look on his face there was no point in arguing with him. She swallowed back her urge to cry. Maybe if she gave him time to cool off she could convince him it was okay for her to live there. He could make repairs if he wanted, but she could stay while they were being done.

They stood there, staring at each other. Finally he cleared his throat and gestured toward the bedroom behind the kitchen where she was currently sleeping. "You can stay here. If you don't feel comfortable with that, I can get you an apartment in town."

Her relief was tempered by the fact he didn't sound pleased with either option, but it was more than Trish had expected.

She was surprised at his offer to stay at the house. She'd gotten the distinct impression when he'd first arrived that he hadn't been pleased to find her here.

Did he mean he'd pay for an apartment? How would she get back and forth? She didn't have transportation, and the bus only ran a few times a day. She knew the schedule by heart, and there was no way she could work here from morning until after dinner and use the bus.

"Trish?" he said, his voice impatient.

She knew he didn't want her here in the house, but he'd given her a choice, so she was going to take the only option that was workable for her. She realized it carried some risk. "I'd like to stay here."

An expression that looked like relief crossed his face. He nodded curtly and headed for the stairs.

Don't be silly, she told herself, knowing she'd misread his reaction. It was nothing personal.

He just wanted her here, in his house, to take care of him.

Nothing personal.

But part of her wanted it to be personal. What a dreamer she was. Ian was a sophisticated, successful man. Why would he ever be interested in a girl like her?

Chapter Seven

Trish was on her hands and knees, head in the oven, scrubbing at the burned-on mess. Last night's lasagna had bubbled over. She was busy calling herself all kinds of fool for not putting the baking dish on a cookie sheet.

Emma was on her tummy on a blanket across the room near the warmth of the furnace vent.

They had officially been living in the main house for three days, and she was trying hard not to get in Ian's way. She had to keep Emma quiet so she wouldn't disturb him and get her work done.

Evenings were the hardest. He started writing around noon and wrote late into the night. She didn't feel comfortable sitting on the couch in the great room doing nothing while he worked, so she kept busy, but it was wearing her down.

She wanted to go back to the stone house in the worst way, but he refused to even discuss the possibility. She didn't want to push the issue and end up commuting from an apartment in town.

"You're working too hard."

Trish jumped at the sound of Ian's voice expressing exactly what she had just been thinking and whacked her head on the top of the oven.

She shifted back out of the oven and, sitting back on her heels, glanced at him over her shoulder.

She tried for a neutral expression on her face and hoped she didn't have oven cleaner in her hair. "It's my job. Besides, I can't use the oven again until I get the burned stuff off."

"It's ten o'clock in the morning. You were working at ten o'clock last night. What happened to the eight-to-five workday?"

He should be the last one to talk about regular hours. She stood up and peeled off the rubber gloves, then shrugged and laughed. "This job is different."

He was looking very annoyed, and she didn't know what else to say. She tamped down the little edge of panic that caught her whenever he seemed angry. She told herself she was so vulnerable to his moods only because she desperately needed the security of this job.

"You don't have to jump up and feel like

you must feed me every time I come downstairs."

"Okay." He was mad about something, but she didn't get the impression it was her. She stopped herself from putting her hand up to cover her racing heartbeat.

He stared at her for a moment. "I want to establish some ground rules."

"Okay." Maybe he was cranky from being cooped up. It was certainly starting to get to her.

"I don't need three meals a day. When I'm working all I need in the middle of the day is a sandwich."

"Okay," she said, a little confused. All she'd been making him for lunch were sandwiches.

He scowled at her. "And stop saying okay to everything I say."

She blinked at his comment and tried to stifle a smile of relief. He was mad, but it definitely wasn't at her. Something else was bothering him.

He put his hands on his hips. "What's so funny?"

She shrugged and bit her lip to keep from smiling. "Do you want me to argue with you?"

"Of course not," he sputtered. "But you could say something besides okay."

She nodded. "Right."

His expression turned more sour.

She was pushing her luck. Hurriedly she said, "I'll plan sandwiches when you want them. Are the regular dinners all right?"

He nodded and stared at her, but she got the odd impression he wasn't looking at *her*.

"I'll go get the rest of your things from the stone house." Without another word he headed for the mud room.

Trish leaned to her right to watch him, wanting to call after him. She could go this afternoon and get what little was left there. Instinct stilled her tongue. He was agitated, and she knew better than to speak up.

He opened the door, and a blast of cold air rushed in. Through the window to the porch she could see him putting on his jacket, gloves and hat.

With angry, jerky movements he lifted the sled down from the hooks on the wall, opened the screen door and tossed it out into the snow. Then he strapped on the snowshoes and waded out into the waist-deep snow.

The whole time, he looked as if he was talking to himself. Trish didn't know what to think. Maybe the cold air would do him some good. She tried to think of a place to hide so she wouldn't be in his path when he returned.

The thought of him opening the drawers to her dresser and packing up her clothes and underwear did not sit well, but she wasn't about to object, given the mood he was in. She really didn't need more than what she had at the main house because she could do laundry whenever she wanted.

Uneasy at his angry mood, she walked over to Emma and rolled her onto her back. "What do you make of that, baby girl?"

Emma cooed and kicked her feet and waved her hands.

"I know," Trish responded, as if Emma had agreed. "He was certainly in a mood."

She hated the fact that she needed to re-assure herself that he was not mad at her.

Trish held up a wooden spoon, and Emma made a grab for it. Trish angled the spoon closer until the baby could grab it. "We'll just stay out of his way until we figure out what's going on."

Trish rolled Emma back onto her tummy and arranged several kitchen utensils within her reach. The baby dropped the wooden spoon and made a grab for a shiny metal measuring cup.

Trish had learned a long time ago not to react to other people's anger. The quieter she became, the less attention she drew to herself. It had been a good lesson to learn in several of the foster homes where she had lived.

She got to her feet and headed back across the room to finish cleaning the oven. Flying under the radar. That's what Lee, one foster brother, had snidely termed what she did, as if he thought she had been performing acts of cowardice.

Acting the way she did had certainly served her better than Lee's defiance had served him, she thought sadly. Survival had been the key, and her method had proved more effective than his.

Trish quickly did a few more chores until Emma began to fuss. She dried her hands and scooped up the baby, carrying her to the couch. After she fed her she would put her down for a nap and stay in the bedroom until Mr. Grumpy was safely back upstairs.

Trish settled in the corner she favored for nursing the baby and when she had Emma started, she picked up the historical romance she and Emma had been reading.

She finished a chapter and shifted Emma

to her other breast, and was settling back into the story when she heard the outside door to the side porch open.

She tensed up and put the book down. She'd thought she would have enough time to feed the baby and clear out before he returned.

She reached back and pulled the afghan from the back of the couch down over the nursing baby, then glanced over her shoulder. Ian was out on the porch stomping the snow off his boots.

After he shrugged out of his coat he came into the house, a bundle tucked under his arm. He looked around the room until he spotted her on the couch and broke into a big grin.

Trish caught her breath. She'd never seen him smile. Heavens, he was one handsome man.

He crossed the room to her in long strides and dropped the bundle on the couch beside her. He'd used her pillowcase as a bag for her things.

Then, still grinning, he leaned forward and cupped her face with his cold hands. He gave her a friendly smack on the mouth that she felt reverberate through her whole body.

"Thanks!" he said, then turned and

strode from the room.

She sat there, staring after him. Her mouth, still tingling from his kiss, hanging open.

What had just happened? He had left as grouchy as a bear interrupted during hibernation, and had come back grinning and then planted a kiss on her lips.

Head spinning, she went over the conversation they'd had before he'd left and came up with nothing.

Her fingertips brushed over her still-sensitive lips, wondering why his trip down to the stone house had caused such a change in him.

She had no idea what had occurred, but she did come up with a conclusion. He should get out more often.

Chapter Eight

Ian took the stairs two at a time, trying to ignore the fact that Trish smelled like sugar cookies and had the softest skin he'd ever touched.

The solution for the story problem he'd run into had occurred to him as he'd unloaded the drawers of Trish's and the baby's things.

That was the way it went for him when he was writing. A character or situation would refuse to jell. It frustrated the hell out of him. Then, at the oddest times, everything would suddenly become clear.

As his fingers flew over the keys of his computer, he was aware the character who had appeared in the story reminded him a lot of Trish. Not that she looked like Trish, but there were things about her, an essence, that was similar.

He didn't stop to consider if it had any significance; he just considered it a gift from his muse. He found if he tried to analyze his writing too much it distracted him from the story and messed up the pacing.

He heard a roaring sound and stopped for a moment to watch a huge county snowplow churn its way up the road. Behind it came a pickup truck with a plow attached to the front that turned off the road to plow the driveway to the house. Ian was disappointed to see the roads cleared.

He loved the feeling of isolation, but it had had to end sooner or later. A contractor was coming this afternoon to give him a bid on renovations for the stone house.

He worked for a few more hours until his back and his brain both needed a break, then gave in to his rumbling stomach and headed down the stairs.

Maybe he'd been mistaken. Perhaps it wasn't Trish who smelled like cookies. Maybe she'd been baking. He needed to check.

He went into the great room and looked around but sensed that the house was empty. Where could she have gone?

He found the answer on the counter. A note informed him Trish had gone to town for groceries and there was a sandwich in the refrigerator. All he had to do if he wanted coffee was to switch on the pot.

Ian studied the round, neat printing on the note with a sense of disappointment that surprised him. Since when did he want someone around when he was writing? A week ago he'd have sworn he wouldn't be able to write with her in the house. Then he'd gone and had the most productive streak he'd had in two years.

He opened the refrigerator and spotted a sandwich on a plate covered with plastic wrap.

How long ago had she left? And why hadn't she come upstairs and mentioned it?

He peeled the plastic wrap off the plate and stood at the counter, looking out at the freshly plowed driveway.

She hadn't mentioned she was leaving because he'd made it very clear she was not to disturb him in any way when he was writing. He remembered the look of alarm on her face when he'd come out of the office while she was sanding the stairs.

He'd have to tell her that rules had exceptions. He wanted to know when she was gone.

As he ate his sandwich he decided he needed to find someone to come in and do the heavy work and maintenance. She took on too much. The house and the cooking were plenty to keep her busy.

While his thoughts wandered, the cat appeared out of nowhere and rubbed up against his leg. Normally he was wary of animals of any kind. They seemed to want more attention than he was ready to give. Surprisingly, he found the cat's presence welcome.

He eyed the feline's sheared-off ears, bobbed tail and scarred head. "What kind of story do you have to tell?" he murmured to the scruffy-looking animal leaving white fur on his dark pants. "That must have been an encounter of the worst kind."

His thoughts drifted back to Trish. When spring came, the work outside would certainly require extra help. Joyce could arrange for the property manager to place an ad to hire a caretaker. He could start in the spring, when the stone house repairs were done.

He finished his sandwich and wandered around downstairs for a few minutes, opening closets and cupboards, exploring his new home. The place was so quiet, so different from the city. It was what he had wanted, but without Trish there it felt too lonely, too isolated.

He stood staring into the fireplace, wondering when that had happened. He *liked* isolated. At least, he always had before.

He nudged the laundry basket she used

as a baby bed with his foot and remembered the crib he'd disassembled and moved out of his office. He'd stored the pieces, along with the mattress, in the smallest bedroom. The thought that Emma could use it hadn't occurred to him at the time.

He went upstairs and carried everything down to the great room, then rummaged around in the utility room until he found a tidy little toolbox.

Just as he finished setting up the crib, he heard the dog barking outside and went to the front window overlooking the lane to the house. He could see Trish in the distance, struggling to push a stroller up the lane.

She didn't have a car. He'd assumed she'd called a cab or a car service.

Why hadn't she called him to come and get her?

He went to the porch door and grabbed a jacket, then headed out to help her. The day had turned a bit warmer, and the ground was mushy with mud and old snow.

He met her halfway down the drive. She was struggling so hard to push the huge, old-fashioned stroller through the slush that she didn't notice him until she almost bumped into him. Her head snapped up as she jerked the stroller to a stop.

She gave him a tentative smile, then turned to the dog, who continued to dance around until she greeted him, sniffed the ground and headed toward the barn, his lack of vision not appearing to be a big hindrance.

Not only did she have the stroller loaded with groceries, she had a large backpack on, dwarfing her small frame.

The baby was laying on her back, surrounded by paper bags, grabbing at a string of brightly colored wooden beads tied across the stroller.

Trish looked like an overloaded pack animal. He couldn't say why, but it annoyed him. "Why didn't you call me?"

She looked at him in surprise. "Call you?"

"Yes. To help," he said, exasperated.

She got that scared look on her face he hated. "You were working."

He made an effort to soften his tone. "I could have taken you into town."

Her features showed a flash of surprise, and she gestured down the road. "I take the bus."

She took a bus to go grocery shopping? She did this every week? He did not understand this woman. Did she ever ask for anything?

He watched as she tried to get the stroller started again, but the wheels had sunk down into the muddy gravel of the driveway.

"Here," he said, annoyed and not knowing why, "give that to me."

She hesitated for a moment, then stepped out of the way and let him take over.

He pushed down on the handle bar and freed the front wheels, then gave the carriage a shove to get it moving.

"The next time you need to go to the store, I'll take you," he said gruffly.

She looked at him, surprise plain on her face. Then a smile began playing around her mouth. He stared at her lips, realizing he had never seen her really smile.

"The three of us would never fit in your car, not to mention the groceries."

"You can take the car then. It has a trunk," he said, in defense of his car. True, it had been designed for speed and not utility, but it could hold a week's groceries.

She looked horrified. "Drive your car? But it's so new. And I don't have a car seat for Emma." She seemed to be scrambling for excuses.

New? What difference did that make? "It's insured. Next time you take the car."

He could tell by the expression on her face he hadn't convinced her.

Pushing the stroller up the muddy drive was almost impossible. He couldn't figure out how she had gotten as far as she had. The thing had wheels designed for smooth concrete, not off-roading under less-than-ideal conditions.

Finally they got to the house and he helped her carry everything in and put it on the counter by the sink. Then he flipped on the coffeepot and stood next to the counter with his hands on his hips.

She put the baby on a blanket on the floor and started to put the groceries away, avoiding his gaze.

He was trying to figure her out. She was unlike any woman he'd ever met. She never complained, never tried to wheedle anything out of him and worked way too hard.

The thought occurred to him again. She never asked for anything.

Trish tried not to look at Ian. He was standing there staring at her and it made her nervous.

Finally he spoke. "What are your days off?"

The question took her by surprise. "I,

uh, don't usually take a day off."

He looked surprised. "Why not?"

"Lots to do here, and not much I want to do in town." She loaded vegetables into the crisper.

Everything in town cost money, including the bus to get there, and she was trying to get her bills paid off.

He continued to watch her as she stowed canned goods in the pantry. "How about family? Do you have family in the area you go to visit?" he asked.

She felt the stab of sadness she always experienced when someone asked that question. "No." She finished putting the meat in the refrigerator and closed the door.

"Where do they live?"

He certainly was persistent. She turned to face him. "I mean, I have no family."

He looked surprised. "Your parents are both dead?"

"I don't know." The answer just popped out, surprising her. Usually she found a way not to respond, because the answer hurt so much. She wondered every day why they had left her and where they had gone.

"What do you mean, you don't know?" He sounded incredulous.

After twenty years the pain should have faded, but it always made her feel raw. "I was abandoned when I was around four." She didn't even know what her real name was. She only remembered being called Baby.

Ian looked distinctly uncomfortable. "I don't know what to say."

People usually didn't when they found out what her childhood had been like. That was another reason she didn't mention it.

She shrugged and gave him a rueful look. "People usually don't."

He studied her intently, making her even more uncomfortable. What he thought of her mattered more than it should.

"Where did you grow up?" he finally asked.

She shrugged, trying to act as though it didn't bother her. "Around Philadelphia. In foster care."

Wishing every day that her parents would come for her. Wanting so much to believe they really loved her and she hadn't been abandoned at all but somehow lost. Which was silly, because she remembered seeing their car drive away. Remembered sitting on the cold concrete all night long waiting for them to come back.

"Did anyone ever find out what had happened to your mother and father?"

"No." The way he asked the question made it sound as if something had prevented them coming back to get her. It was a version of the possibilities she'd always liked best. It felt so much better than the thought that she hadn't been lovable enough for them to bother to come back.

"That must have been hard." He shook his head. "Four years old," he said, more to himself than to her.

She put the last of the groceries away, hoping he wouldn't ask any more questions. It was certainly a subject she didn't care to dwell on.

She straightened up, closed the cupboard door and headed toward the utility room with a box of laundry detergent.

The antique metal crib that had been in his office stood by the door to the utility room.

She turned to look at him.

"You need to get the baby out of that basket," he said gruffly.

"You set this up for Emma?" The gesture seemed out of character for him. It touched her in a way she couldn't describe.

"Yes." He made a dismissive gesture with

his hand. "I'll help you move it into your room."

"Thank you." She wanted to say more, but by his brusque manner she could tell he didn't want to hear it.

As they placed the crib by her bed she heard the sound of a vehicle coming up the driveway. The noise interrupted the awkward moment.

"That's probably the contractor. He's going to give me a bid on the stone house." He looked relieved to go as he headed for the front door.

She followed him out of her room and watched him go, torn by emotions. He'd provided a bed for her baby. A valuable antique. She ran her hand along the closely-spaced spindles that made up the sides. To him it might be no big deal, but to her it meant a lot.

Then she thought about where he was going. She knew the stone house needed improvements, but the idea didn't sit well. She thought of it as her home. If he fixed it up it wouldn't be the same. Better, but not the same.

Or would it be too good for her? Things that were too good never came to her.

She laughed to herself. That was just being silly, she thought. If he fixed the house up and it was better, it would still be home for her and Emma.

Wouldn't it?

She tried to ignore her uneasiness. Ian had made it clear from the beginning he wanted her back in the stone house. So what did she have to worry about?

Chapter Nine

Trish tiptoed past Ian's office door, her hands full of clean sheets and towels. She could see him, his back to her, his broad shoulders hunched over his work. The only noise coming from his office was the quiet tapping sound his fingers made as he worked on his keyboard.

She stood staring at him for a moment, realizing this was the first time he'd left the door open as he worked. Before tonight it had always been closed when he was writing.

He straightened up and stretched, and Trish watched as his sweater stretched across the muscles of his back, eyeing him with a kind of yearning she'd never felt before.

He pushed back from the desk and started to turn toward the door. Trish scooted down the hall and into the spare room at the end of the hall where she stored the linens. The last thing she wanted was to be caught drooling over him.

She heard him go downstairs and waited for a moment, then followed him down.

She found him in the kitchen, pouring himself a cup of coffee. The first few days he'd worked he'd taken a Thermos upstairs with him, but lately he'd been coming down when he wanted a fresh cup.

She cleared her throat and he turned to look at her, then glanced at the digital time display on the microwave. "I thought you'd be in bed."

She shrugged. "I'm just about finished." She gestured to his cup. "That's not very fresh. Do you want me to make another pot?"

He stared at her for a long moment, until she had to stop the urge to squirm.

Fresh coffee. It wasn't such a difficult question, she thought. It unnerved her when he stared at her like that.

Finally he blinked. "Sure. I'll be writing for a while." Then he tilted his head just a little and stared at her again.

She went to the counter, shut off the coffeemaker and put the carafe in the sink. She turned on the hot water and glanced at him. He was still watching her.

"Can I get you something to eat?"

He seemed to come out of his trance, and he rubbed his hand over his flat belly.

"No. I'm still full from dinner. That was a great pot roast." He turned and headed back upstairs.

Trish rinsed the coffeepot and turned it upside down on the drainer. He did that a lot, just stared at her. But she got the feeling that he was not really looking at her, but rather trying to figure something out, and she just happened to be his focal point.

It wasn't creepy or anything, just a little strange. His mind seemed miles away sometimes. She supposed it was the way writers worked. In order to create stories, they must always be thinking of something else.

She filled the basket of the coffeemaker with fresh grounds. He drank too much coffee, but she certainly wasn't in a position to lecture him.

She was getting used to his routine. He worked until very late at night, then slept late in the morning.

That worked out well for her, because she could get up early and catch a shower before Emma woke, then feed the baby and bathe and dress her and get some chores done. She would nurse Emma again and put her down for her morning nap. By then it was time to cook his breakfast. The baby usually woke after Ian had gone upstairs and Trish had finished the dishes.

She would put Emma in her infant activity seat and carry her from room to room as she cleaned, or put her in the front pack she could strap to her chest and take her out to the barn to look in on Max.

She'd feed Emma again and put the baby down for an afternoon nap while she prepared lunch, and Ian ate so late that by the time she had to fix dinner, Emma was down for the night.

She had the baby part handled. It was the animals she was worried about. So far Ian hadn't said anything more about getting rid of the horse, but she knew it would come up again.

She kept Crew and Tollie out of the house. They seemed content to share the barn with Max, and everything in the house was running smoothly, but Trish still didn't feel safe.

She worried a lot that something would happen that Ian didn't like and he would want to find a new housekeeper. She had no contract to work, just a verbal agreement, and technically that had been made with the previous owners.

The last thing Trish would do before she went to bed was set up the coffeepot and switch it on, so the coffee would be fresh when he came down for another cup.

Wearily she changed into her pajamas and an old flannel robe. She decided to read for just a little while before bed, but wanted to do it in the great room where it was warmer. She knew Ian's schedule well enough to know he'd write for at least an hour before he came down for another cup of coffee.

She curled up on the couch in front of the fire, her book in her lap. She was warm and cozy and pleasantly tired from a long, satisfying day of work. The biography of Benjamin Franklin was fascinating, but her thoughts kept drifting to Ian.

She thought about the way he'd charged out of the house to meet her down the driveway as she came home from the grocery store. How he had acted angry with her and insisted on taking over the stroller and pushing it to the house.

A small gesture, perhaps, but the kind of thing that made him seem like a hero to her. No one had ever taken care of her before or seemed concerned for her comfort.

She leaned her head against the soft pillow at the back of the couch. What would it be like to belong to a man like Ian? Someone who would help her with the little things. Sometimes she got so lonely. Ian had the money to keep her safe from the world, to keep Emma comfortable and give her daughter all the things Trish had never had.

Like dance lessons. Trish closed her eyes and remembered a time when she had been around eight. She'd been on her way home from a trip to the drugstore to pick up some things for her foster mother. There was a dance studio in the strip mall and a group of girls about her age were coming out of a class. They were all wearing pink tights and leotards and filmy little skirts. Even their slippers were pink. She'd watched them laughing and giggling together.

She'd never worn pastel colors as a child. They weren't practical. Showed the dirt too much. The foster homes usually had boxes of hand-me-downs, and she would try to find clothes that fit. There was never anything frilly or pink. Most of the time the clothes were worn jeans and T-shirts, suitable for either a boy or girl.

The girls from the dancing school had gotten into cars, where their mothers had been waiting for them out front.

No one had ever waited for Trish.

Trish sighed. After that day she'd taken

the long way home to that foster home whenever she'd been sent on errands.

What would it be like to belong to someone? Someone who cared. Again Ian floated into her thoughts. What a fool she was. Men like Ian Miller didn't want women like her. They wanted someone with style and sophistication. Someone with an education. The image of Joyce Sommers came to mind. That was the kind of woman Ian Miller would choose.

Ian came down for a cup of coffee and saw that the coffeemaker hadn't been switched on. It wasn't like Trish to forget, but she must have gone to bed without turning it on.

He flipped the switch and leaned against the counter. Usually she was so efficient he didn't have to think about anything. He appreciated that in his housekeeper. It helped to make his writing time more productive.

The coffee sizzled and sputtered, then began to flow into the glass pot, the aroma rich and heady. It bothered him that she worked such long hours, but she seemed to get a little panicked when he'd tried to discuss it with her. She never took any time off.

Ian heard a soft rustling noise coming from the couch that faced the fireplace. Perhaps one of the animals had gotten in. He walked over and looked over the back, expecting to see the cat or the dog curled up on the cushions.

Instead he found Trish. She had a book in her lap and she was sound asleep with her head on one of the pillows. Her curly blond hair was tousled and her eyelashes fanned over her cheeks. He remembered what she had told him about being abandoned.

What did that do to a person? To be discarded at such a tender age, like an old piece of furniture no one wanted? It was amazing she was usually so cheerful.

His own parents tended to be cold and aloof, but he had felt secure as a child. They didn't demonstrate their feelings outwardly, but he had always been cared for.

He leaned over the couch and gently pulled the book from her limp hands. She stirred and burrowed into the pillow but didn't wake.

He walked around to the front of the couch and put the book on the table, then went back to watching her sleep. In her oversize flannel robe and bare feet she looked adorable.

What might she do if he kissed her to wake her up? He was tempted to pick her up and carry her to her bed. And he certainly wouldn't be averse to joining her there.

He stepped back, appalled at his thoughts.

She was his housekeeper, not his girlfriend. Recently widowed and obviously dependent on him for her job, the last thing she needed was to know he was attracted to her. It would put her in a terrible position.

It must be the book he was working on, he thought, trying desperately to explain his errant thoughts. The new character, the one that was guiding the action, was based on Trish. He'd refused to admit it for a while, but now it was so obvious he could no longer deny it.

The physical description of his new character in the book wasn't like Trish, but the spirit and heart of her reminded him of his housekeeper.

Trish looked like an angel, but he had sensed in her a core of steel. He had no doubt she would fight to the death to protect what was important to her. For Trish that was Emma.

Did he have anything he cared so much

about? He didn't think so, and the thought made him strangely sad.

He hadn't even realized his story needed a female character, but the story had begun to flow when he'd introduced her into the text.

That explained his feelings, he decided. He was always attracted to his characters. This was just the first time he'd modeled a character after a real person.

The coffeepot beeped, signaling the brewing stage was done. Trish's eyes fluttered, and Ian moved back across to the kitchen side of the room.

He turned at her soft muttering and saw her sit up and blink at him. For a moment she looked confused, then she scrambled to her feet.

"I, uh, I was just reading."

She looked even cuter awake. "You were sleeping. Go to bed." He turned to pour his coffee, realizing he'd sounded harsher than he'd intended, but he didn't like this growing attraction to her.

He didn't care that she was sleeping, but he did care that he'd been tempted to kiss her while she did it.

"Yes. I will." She hurried past him into the small room beyond the kitchen. He waited until he heard the quiet sound of

117

the door closing before he headed back up-stairs, mentally kicking himself for the way he had handled that little scene.

He was much better at dealing with his characters than he was with real people.

Trish had tried harder than ever this morning to stay out of Ian's way. He had obviously been annoyed to find her asleep on the couch last night.

She wiped down the counter, glancing over at him occasionally. All she could see was the back of his head as he sat on the couch and watched CNN while he ate his lunch.

There was some breaking news on televi-sion, and Ian seemed intent on the screen. She wished he'd go back upstairs so she could get out to the barn to take care of Max before Emma woke up. She hadn't had a chance this morning, and she needed to check the horse's leg. He seemed to be favoring it more than usual.

It was so much easier to work without the baby, and with the monitor and Ian in the house, Trish felt comfortable leaving her for a short period of time.

"Where's the baby?"

Ian's voice startled her. She pointed to the hall that led to the utility room and her bedroom. "She's still asleep."

"Isn't she usually awake by now?"

His question surprised Trish. She hadn't been aware he even noticed the baby.

"Usually. But she went down for her nap a little later than she normally does."

Ian used the remote to switch off the television, then stood and stretched, his sweater pulling over his arms and shoulders. Trish turned away so she wouldn't be tempted to stare.

He had beautiful clothes and a lovely body to hang them on. The sweater he had on was cashmere. She'd peeked at the tag when she'd folded it up while tidying his room. It was a lovely off-white shade that was totally impractical for a dry-clean-only sweater, but it looked good with his dark hair.

He finished his stretch and shook his head. "She really has the life. Eat, sleep and play. No wonder we don't remember being babies. We'd never want to grow up."

A wave of gloom washed over Trish. She wished she remembered being a baby. She wanted to know her mother and father, and whether they'd even loved her.

"Hey, what's wrong?"

She blinked and realized he'd moved

across the room toward her, plate in hand.

"Nothing. Here, let me take that." She'd already made him uncomfortable enough telling him about being abandoned.

He watched her for a few heartbeats, then said, "Back to work." He turned and headed for the stairs.

Trish stashed the dirty dishes in the sink. She tiptoed into her room and peeked at Emma, who was sound asleep. If she went straight to the barn, she thought as she hung the baby monitor on the crib, she could feed Max, check his leg and be back in a few minutes, before Emma woke and needed to eat again.

Ian came back downstairs. He had been so absorbed trying to figure out why Trish had looked so sad all of a sudden that he'd forgotten to get a fresh cup of coffee to take upstairs.

When he'd seen her go out to the barn just now, he decided it would be a good time to go downstairs. This way she wouldn't think he was an idiot for forgetting, or guess he was attracted to her and kept coming down just to see her. He didn't like either alternative.

Exhausted, he needed the coffee. He'd been up almost all night writing. The story had flowed so fast he could hardly keep up with it.

It was never a good idea to question your muse, but he wondered how long she was going to hang around. He'd never had such a run of good, productive writing, but he needed some sleep.

He heard an indignant howl from the direction of Trish's room. He put the empty mug down and walked down the short hallway to the room where she and the baby slept.

Except Emma wasn't asleep.

When he bent over and peered into the little bed, the miniature version of Trish gave him a toothless smile and waved her little hands in the air, as if she was glad to see him.

To test his assumption, he straightened up and took a step back, and her little face seemed to crumple. She squinted up her eyes and the corners of her tiny mouth turned down in a pout of such female outrage it made him smile.

He leaned back over the crib, and again the baby grinned at him.

Ian was uncomfortable with the prospect of tears, even from a baby. Not knowing quite what to do, he extended his index finger to her. She switched her gaze from his face to his finger, and for a moment eyed it with intense concentration, as if it was the most interesting thing she'd ever seen. Then she brought her hand up and made a grab for him, closing her tiny hand around his finger.

He stood like that for a moment, watching her. He tried to pull his finger away, but she had a better grip than he had anticipated.

With his other hand he picked up a plastic rattle that was down by her feet and waved that in front of her. She let go of his finger and grabbed at the brightly colored plastic. Ian was vaguely disappointed that she preferred the toy to him.

The outside porch door slammed and Ian straightened up. He heard Trish coming down the hall.

She stopped in the doorway when she saw him standing by the crib.

She immediately looked very uncomfortable and said in a rush as she hurried into the room, "I just ran out to the barn to check on Max."

She gestured to the baby with the monitor she held in her hand. "I didn't hear her cry." She frowned at the monitor, then looked back up at him. "Did she disturb you?"

"Not at all." He gestured to the monitor in her hand. "It probably needs new batteries. I came down for coffee and she was awake." He tried to tell if he had offended her by getting too close to the baby without her permission. "Do you mind if I talk to her?"

A surprised expression flashed across Trish's face. "Oh, no. Not at all," she said in a rush. Trish slid a hand under the baby's head and lifted her out of the bed. "I just don't want you to be bothered."

Ian shrugged, secretly flattered that she, so protective of her child, trusted him. "She's no bother. In fact, when you have to go outside, let me know. That way I can listen for her and you don't have to worry about her."

He amazed himself as he heard the words coming out of his mouth. Ian Miller, confirmed bachelor, had just offered to baby-sit. Not for any long period of time, but still, if anyone had told him he'd be doing that a month ago he'd have laughed out loud.

Next thing he knew, he'd be writing a baby into his story.

"I've got to get back." He quickly left her room, poured a mug of coffee and headed back upstairs.

Instead of going directly back to work, he leaned back in his chair and thought about Emma. He remembered her birth date from the tiny hospital announcement taped to the wall in the stone farmhouse. He counted back. She must be close to four months old.

He connected with the Internet and searched until he found a Web site that gave week-by-week detailed information about babies and what to expect. He read what was offered and decided Emma was advanced for her age, on top of being the prettiest baby he'd ever seen. He bookmarked the site and went back to his writing.

Chapter Ten

Trish was dragging a heavy load of wet towels from the washer to the dryer when she heard Ian calling her name.

She dropped the towels and raced to the bottom of the stairs, but then she realized his voice was coming from out front, from the driveway.

She stuck her head out the front door and was greeted by a blast of cold air. Ian was standing with a middle-aged man by a bright red truck in the curve of the driveway.

He caught sight of her and gestured to her. "Get your jacket and come out."

Trish nodded and closed the door, wondering who the man was and why Ian didn't invite him in out of the cold.

As she went through the great room to the porch to get her jacket, she did a mental inventory.

The coffee was freshly made. She could make sandwiches if Ian wanted to invite the visitor to lunch. On the way out she checked Emma. The baby was still sound asleep.

Trish put on her jacket and left the room, then made a detour back by the crib to get the baby monitor, tucking it in the pocket of her jacket.

When she opened the front door there was a van coming up the front drive. It pulled up behind the truck.

Aside from the contractor, Ian hadn't had any visitors since he arrived and now he had two. If these men were going to be working on the stone house, she wondered why Ian needed her.

The man by the truck handed Ian something, then shook his hand and headed for the van.

Ian spotted her and gestured for her to come over. When she got about ten feet from him he said, "What do you think?"

She looked at him and then at the two men pulling away in the van. "About what?" she asked, puzzled over the whole scene.

He held up his hand. A silver key dangled from his fingers. "The truck. I bought it for the farm. You can use it to get to town. You know, to shop."

Trish stared at the key as if he were trying to hypnotize her with it. He'd bought a truck for her to use. It was the sweetest thing anyone had ever done for her.

Ian looked alarmed and backed up a step. "Are you going to cry?"

The red of the truck blurred, and she realized her eyes were welling with tears. "No. It's just that . . . I . . . don't know what to say." Don't you cry, she told herself firmly, whatever you do, don't cry.

He kept one wary eye on her as he opened the truck's door. She leaned into the cab, her hand brushing over the beige leather upholstery. She inhaled the surprisingly pleasant aroma. She'd never been in a new vehicle before. It was wonderful. In fact, she thought, it was one of the best smells she'd ever experienced. It seemed to go to her head and make her giddy.

She stepped up onto the running board to get a better look. The roomy interior had a bench seat behind the bucket seats. In the middle of the back seat sat a brand-new infant car seat.

Trish fell in love with him, right there, standing on the running board of his shiny new truck. How could she not love a man who would do something like this? She didn't care that he was gruff and grumpy and totally unattainable. She was going to love him and it would be her little secret.

She ran her hand over the fresh plaid fabric of the pad in the infant seat, then turned to Ian. He was now eye level with her. "Ian, now I'm going to cry."

He looked panic-stricken. It was just what she needed to stop her tears and make her realize how silly she was being to love him. She laughed as she scrambled up onto the seat.

The truck was wonderful, but her feet didn't touch the pedals. She grinned down at him. "I think they built this one for the big boys."

He looked relieved at her smile. "The seat is adjustable," he said quickly. "The pedals are, too." He took her left hand and guided it down to a lever on the side of the seat. "It adjusts right here.

"Pull it up to bring the seat higher, and forward to bring you in closer to the steering wheel."

While she fiddled with the adjustment, he crouched down by the open door and pulled a lever under the dashboard. Then he grabbed her ankle and placed her foot on the brake. "How does that feel?"

Wonderful, she wanted to say. She loved the feel of his hands on her. But he was talking about the change he'd made.

She settled back against the seat and gripped the wheel. "It's good. I can see fine and reach the brake and accelerator."

He held out the key. "Here. Take it for a drive."

Startled at his offer, she started to get out. "I couldn't. It's brand-new."

He looked exasperated and put his hand on her arm to stop her. "Of course it's brand-new. I just bought it."

What if she got a dent in it. Or worse, had an accident. "But . . . I've never driven a new car."

He gave her a wry look. "It's pretty much the same as driving an old car."

"But what if something happens? What if it gets a dent or a scratch or a dent or . . ."

"Trish, I bought it to use around the farm. It *will* get dents and scratches."

"But . . ."

"Do you want me to drive it right now and bang it up? I could brush it by the low branch on the tree behind the barn. Get a few scratches on it. Would you feel okay to drive it then?"

She couldn't tell if he was amused or annoyed. She sighed. "You think I'm being silly."

Ian nodded. "Yes, pretty much."

"It's just that I've never been in a new car before. I have a license, but I don't have a lot of experience driving."

Suddenly there was a squawk from the monitor in her pocket. "Emma's waking up." She grabbed at the excuse and jumped out of the truck.

The only problem was Ian didn't back up and she landed on him. He grabbed her, so they both wouldn't fall, and held her for a long moment. Then he let her go when her feet touched the ground.

Her heart was pounding so hard she was surprised she could draw a breath.

He put some distance between them. When he tried to speak he had to clear his throat. Finally he managed, "Go get Emma. We'll go for a ride."

Trish wanted to touch him so much she backed up three steps to break the temptation. "But —"

He made a frustrated gesture with his hand. "Trish, go get Emma."

She hated the thought of keeping him waiting. "It will take a while. I have to change her and —"

He laughed, grabbed her by the shoulders and turned her toward the house, then gave her a gentle push. "Go!"

Trish ran back to the house. She scooped Emma out of her crib just as Emma had her face all screwed up into a look of outrage.

Abruptly she smiled and gurgled. Trish nuzzled her cheek. "Did you think I'd left you?" She held the baby out so she could see her beautiful little face. "I'll never leave you. Never," she said fiercely.

She carried her into the utility room and put her on the pad on top of the dryer she used as a changing table.

"We're going for a ride in Mr. Miller's new truck." Emma gurgled her approval. "You have a new baby seat and everything."

She couldn't believe Ian had been so thoughtful. If he didn't mind her driving once a week, her errands to town could all be done in a morning. It would save her hours of time. She could do the grocery shopping and pick up his dry cleaning and feed for Max, all at the same time.

She pulled the tiny fleece jacket on over Emma's overalls and T-shirt. When she pulled the zipper up, Emma looked like a fat little pink sausage. She could also go to the thrift shop and see if they had some winter baby clothes in a bigger size. Emma was growing so quickly all the things she had were getting too small.

With Emma hoisted over her shoulder, she grabbed a baby blanket and the small bag she used as a purse, locked the front door and carried Emma out to the truck.

Ian sat in the passenger seat, looking at the owner's manual. He looked up and then laid the book on the console.

He hopped down out of the truck and came around and showed Trish the handle recessed in the side of the door that opened to the back seat.

She tossed her bag in, then climbed up with Emma and laid her in the car seat, adjusting the straps until they fit snugly over her chest.

She jumped down and closed the door, then headed around the side of the truck to the passenger seat.

Ian caught her by the arm. "Oh, no. You're going to drive." He spun her around so she was headed toward the open driver's door.

She looked over her shoulder at him. "This first time I think you should drive."

He shook his head. "The seat and the pedals are all adjusted for you." He pointed to the door, then walked around the back of the truck.

She climbed up on the running board, slid into the seat and fumbled nervously with the seat belt buckle. Her hands were so damp with perspiration she had trouble with the latch before she finally got it to click shut.

She looked over at Ian. He had his seat belt fastened and was staring at her intently. "You're afraid, aren't you?"

Trish thought about acting brave and denying it, but she was terrible at fibbing. "Yes."

Ian continued to stare for a moment, then his expression softened. "Were you in the car when your husband was killed?" he asked in a concerned tone.

She had a flash memory of the night the state trooper had knocked on her door at four in the morning to tell her about the accident. She shook her head. "No. I was home with Emma."

He put his hand on her shoulder. "I want you to drive, but if it's too much for you, I understand."

The warmth of his palm and his gentle, caring tone made Trish want to unbuckle her seat belt and climb across the console into his lap. She knew she'd feel safe there.

Instead she gripped the steering wheel and said, "I'm okay."

She hadn't been thinking of the accident at all. She'd been thinking of the pretty red paint on the new truck, and how she'd feel if she got a scratch on it.

"Okay. The key is in the ignition." She leaned to her right and saw the big black plastic handle of the key sticking out of the ignition lock.

She glanced back at Emma, who was wide-eyed as she looked around. Trish grasped the key and twisted it. The engine started right up and rumbled reassuringly.

Ian pointed out the gearshift, the instrument panel on the dash, the control to switch to four-wheel drive and the gas gauge.

"Do you have a credit card that is earmarked for expenses for the farm?"

Trish nodded, wondering why he was asking that now. "The bills go to your accountant, I think, but I have a ledger. I keep track of everything I spend."

"When you need to fill the tank, use the credit card. It has dual tanks, so you shouldn't have to do it too often. You feel ready?"

As ready as she'd ever feel. "Sure." She tried to sound confident, but her palms were still sweating.

Ian pointed to the driveway out front. "Let's go."

"Okay." She eased the gearshift into drive. "Where do you want to go?" She maneuvered down the driveway, carefully avoiding a rut that had appeared after the last storm.

Ian rubbed his hand over his stomach. "Let's go into town and get some lunch."

Just like that, he wanted to go out to eat. The thought made her a little giddy. This was a whole new thing. She knew how to be his housekeeper and his cook, but she wasn't sure how to go out to lunch with him.

"I'm not dressed to go out." She looked down at her old corduroy coat and jeans. Clean, but definitely worn.

Ian shrugged. "We'll find a casual place. No problem."

Trish turned onto the road that headed toward town. "There's a truck stop on the highway about five miles from here." As soon as the words were out of her mouth, she realized someone like Ian wouldn't want to eat at a truck stop.

She glanced over and was surprised to see him nod. "A truck stop? Perfect. I hear they have the best food."

She shot him a sideways glance, not daring to take her eyes off the road for more than a second. "That is a highly exaggerated rumor."

She'd eaten at plenty of truck stops, and the only thing they had in common was that truckers stopped there, not good food.

But if Ian wanted a truck stop, she'd give him one.

She heard a horn honking and glanced in the rearview mirror. She was surprised to see three cars behind her. "There usually isn't a lot of traffic on this road."

Ian looked over his shoulder and laughed. "Maybe they just caught up with you. You're only going fifteen miles an hour."

She glanced at the speedometer and winced. She'd been trying so hard to be careful she hadn't realized how slowly she was going.

"The speed limit along here is forty. You can give it a little gas."

Trish speeded up and then slowed to make the turn onto the highway. They rolled along in companionable silence. She signaled and turned into the parking lot of the truck stop.

The *S* in the neon sign that read Tiny's Good Eats was flickering off and on. The cinder-block front of the diner was stained with streaks of rust where metal brackets fastened the sign to the building.

Trish braked to a stop and viewed the place with a critical eye. It certainly wasn't the kind of place Ian Miller would eat.

"Let's go somewhere else."

"No. this is perfect. Pull in over there and park." He pointed to a spot beside the Dumpster.

Reluctantly she pulled into the parking space and put the truck in park. She glanced back at Emma, who was sound asleep. The motion of the ride must have lulled her back into a second nap.

Trish pocketed the keys, then went around to the back seat and unfastened the seat belt securing the infant safety seat. She scooted Emma to the edge of the seat, then lifted the whole thing out.

Ian came up behind her and closed the truck's doors. Trish carried Emma to the door of the restaurant. Ian opened the heavy glass door and held it for her.

They were greeted by a rush of sounds and smells. Mournful country music, the rumble of men's voices, the heavy scent of fried food and onions.

The walls held an assortment of stuffed animal heads, dusty framed photographs and ancient farm implements. An impressive network of spiderwebs connected everything.

A waitress approached and Trish glanced up at Ian. "Are you sure —"

He held up a hand. "It's perfect."

Trish watched the approaching waitress admire Ian. The only perfect thing in the place was him.

The waitress showed them to a booth and handed them each a sticky plastic-covered menu. Trish put Emma, still sound asleep despite the noise and lights, into the corner of the booth. This was so *not* an Ian Miller place, she realized, embarrassed she'd ever thought he would want to eat here.

As she took off her jacket and slid in beside Emma, she looked up to see Ian still standing. Perhaps he was having second thoughts. Then he sat and she realized he was just being polite and waiting for her to sit first.

She picked up the menu and opened it, not reading the words but marveling over his manners.

As far as she could remember, no man had ever waited for her to be seated. The only time she had seen men practice the old-fashioned custom was in the black-and-white movies from the forties showing on late-night TV.

She studied him as he studied the menu. His dark hair was thick and beautifully cut. Full eyelashes outlined incredible blue eyes.

He looked up and caught her studying him. Embarrassed, she looked down at her menu.

"Well?"

She looked up at him. "What?"

He gestured to the menu. "What do you want for lunch?"

"Oh. A hamburger, please." It would be a treat to eat a meal she hadn't prepared and wouldn't have to clean up.

The hamburgers weren't too expensive, and she supposed he would pay the check, but she wasn't sure.

The waitress headed for their table. Ian took the menu from Trish and, with a smooth gesture, handed the plastic folders to the waitress and ordered their food as if they were in an elegant restaurant.

As they made small talk, Trish watched his refined manners and confidence, wondering what it would be like to go through life expecting to get what you wanted, all the time.

The waitress returned with thick crockery plates filled with huge hamburgers and mounds of fries. Ian kept looking around the place as if he were fascinated by the experience as he ate. Trish supposed he'd never been to a truck stop before.

He gestured in general to their surroundings. "This place is perfect."

Curiosity got the better of her and she had to ask. "For what?"

He pushed his plate away and gave her a sheepish smile that was very appealing. "For my book. I needed a place for the protagonist to meet with the hired killer. I think this will do it."

She smiled. That explained his fascination with a rather ordinary truck stop.

Before she could think of something to say, he slid out of the booth. "I need to see what the bathroom looks like."

Trish nodded, unable to think of an appropriate response. If it was the usual public rest room, it would look as if it needed a good cleaning. Would he put that in a book? she wondered as she watched him walk away. Several other women, from a teenager in a booth across from them to a gray-haired woman at the cash register also watched him.

Emma stirred and yawned. Trish leaned over the car seat and Emma gave her a big smile, then suddenly seemed to remember she'd missed a meal. Her face collapsed into what Trish liked to think of her "Oh, poor me" look. Trish had hoped her daughter would sleep until they got back to the farm so she could feed her there, but Emma apparently had other plans.

Trish's choice was to feed the baby here or subject Ian to her crying all the way home. It really wasn't much of a choice. She plucked the baby out of the seat, draped a blanket over her shoulder and Emma, then arranging the baby's blanket over the both of them for a little privacy, she opened her shirt and settled her at her breast.

Ian returned from his exploration of the men's room and slid back into the booth.

"Are you done eating?" He glanced down at her plate, which was completely empty except for a slice of onion she'd pulled off her burger. "I guess you are. Want anything else?"

She shook her head. "I'm full." She glanced down at the baby. "Are you in a hurry to get back?"

For the first time Ian seemed to notice she was holding the baby under the blanket.

"Oh, no. No, go ahead and finish feeding her." His eyes immediately left her to look around the room. Anywhere but at her.

He was blushing.

Trish fought back a smile. The urbane, sophisticated man actually blushed. She thought it was sweet. Then a thought occurred to her. He was probably embarrassed. She doubted that women he spent time with would nurse a baby in public.

The waitress came back, asked if they wanted anything else, then left their check. Ian rolled up on one hip to dig his wallet out of his pocket, then he looked embarrassed. "I didn't bring my wallet. Do you have the farm credit card?"

"Sure." One-handed she pulled her wallet out of the diaper bag and slid the credit card out of its slot, handing it to him.

"I'll go pay the bill. Will you . . . uh, Emma be finished soon?"

"She's about done." Emma had enough in her tummy to hold her for a while. Trish could finishing feeding her at home. She put the baby back in the car seat and met Ian at the register. At least she hadn't had to face the awkwardness of talking about splitting the bill.

She followed Ian out to the truck, dug the key out of her pocket and handed it to him. He unlocked the truck and opened up the doors, then, as she put the baby in the back seat, he stood staring at the cinderblock building that housed Tiny's.

"Ian? Do you want to drive?"

He seemed to come out of his trance. "You go ahead." He went around and climbed into the passenger seat.

All the way home he read the manual and fiddled with the clock and set the radio buttons. "What kind of music do you like?"

Trish shrugged. "Almost any kind. Would you mind setting one of the buttons for NPR?"

He looked a little surprised. "You like public radio?"

Did he think she was too uneducated to appreciate the programs? She gripped the steering wheel and stared out the windshield. "Yes, I do."

"No problem," he said as she turned onto Blacksmith Farm Road.

As they came up the driveway, Trish noticed the car parked in the curve of the drive by the front door. The driver was sitting in the car.

Ian groaned. "Joyce. I forgot she was coming."

Trish pulled up beside the barn, and Ian jumped out of the passenger door.

Trish got the baby out and slowly followed him to the house.

She could tell by her body language Joyce Sommers was angry when she got out of her car. She stood facing Ian with her arms crossed over an elegant black wool suit. "Ian. We had an appointment."

Ian gave her his charming little-boy grin that didn't seem to achieve the desired effect. "Sorry, Joyce. We went out for lunch."

She looked mad enough to spit nails. She seemed to struggle for control, then she pivoted on her stylish high heels and plucked a folder and a small handbag off the seat of the car.

"I tried your cell several times." Her tone was still tight and angry.

Ian shrugged, apparently not very impressed with her show of anger. "I didn't take it with me."

Joyce made an exasperated gesture with her perfectly manicured hand. "For heaven's sake, Ian. What good is a cell phone if you're not going to carry it?"

"I never wanted the thing in the first place. It was your idea." Trish could tell by Ian's tone he was losing patience.

Trish, feeling very awkward, walked past the couple and unlocked the front door.

Joyce glanced over at Trish. "Hello, Tina."

"Trish." Ian and Trish corrected Joyce at the same time.

Trish stepped into the house. She had

the distinct impression the woman had gotten her name wrong on purpose. A not-so-subtle reminder that Joyce did not find her worth remembering.

Joyce walked through the door, and her gaze settled on Emma. "What is that?"

Ian took Joyce by the elbow and led her into the house. "It's called a baby, Joyce. Most humans start life that way."

Trish couldn't hear the rest of their conversation as Ian led her upstairs to his office.

She carried Emma to the couch and finished feeding her daughter. She could hear the murmur of conversation coming from Ian's office.

She couldn't help but make the comparison between herself and Joyce. Joyce, in her designer clothes and stylish haircut and manicure would never be caught dead in a place like Tiny's. Trish, in her flannel shirt and jeans would probably never eat anywhere nicer.

As much as she hated to admit it, Joyce was much more Ian's type. She just hoped he'd find someone nicer. He deserved more.

Ian finished signing the papers Joyce had brought and listened patiently as she went over the details of what she kept referring to as a "very important party." It was actually the premiere for a new movie based on his fifth novel, and he knew it was more for the studio than it was for him.

At least she had passed the stage of showing her claws and hissing at him. He'd forgotten all about her coming today. The business end of his career drove him mad, and he tended to ignore it whenever he could. That's why he paid Joyce a huge salary to deal with it.

As she discussed who would be there, he found himself wondering if Trish would like to attend. He doubted she'd ever been to a movie premiere. Most people hadn't. She might enjoy seeing the stars and the glittering show the studio would make of the night.

"And so I'll book your ticket and make sure you have a suite at the Wilshire Grand."

"Whoa. Wait. The party is on the West Coast?" He didn't want to travel that far for a party, and he wasn't sure about Trish and the baby.

The flight might be too much for Emma. How old did a baby have to be to fly? He'd heard them crying on planes, but they were never in first class so he didn't know if they were as young as Emma.

Joyce gave him a blank look. "Well, of course the premiere is in California."

"But the last one was in New York."

She shook her head and gave him a "Why don't you ever pay attention?" look. "That was for your last book launch, Ian."

Her arms were crossed over her chest and her foot was tapping a staccato little rhythm on the hardwood floor. Not a good sign.

Now that he had the idea, he wanted to take Trish to a party. "When's my next book party?"

She threw her hands up and gave him an incredulous look. "You insisted you didn't want a launch party for your next book."

He vaguely remembered that conversation. "But you thought it was a good idea."

"I thought it was an *excellent* idea."

He shrugged. "So let's do it."

She sputtered, "Ian, the book comes out in three weeks!"

This reminded him he was way behind schedule on the book he was writing. He'd like to have the manuscript he was working on finished before his next book came out in print.

He took her by the arm and led her downstairs and out the front door. "You can pull it off. I know you can. Just tell my editor and publisher, book a restaurant in New York and let them pull it together."

She dug in her heels as he tried to get her out the front door. "Will you attend the party in L.A.?"

He knew her negotiating tactics. If he wanted the launch in New York, he'd have to attend the Hollywood premiere.

"Okay. But book me on a red-eye both ways. I don't want to be out there for more than two days."

She started to complain, then Ian cut her off.

"Two days, Joyce. I need to be here to work."

"There will be people you need to see."

"No." He shook his head, made a cutting motion with his hand. He watched Joyce stomp to her car and realized the only two people he wanted to see were right here, at Blacksmith Farm.

Chapter Eleven

Trish stood in the dark at the front window and watched the taillights of Ian's car disappear down the driveway. Suddenly the house that had always been so warm and cozy had an empty feel.

He was only going to be on the West Coast for two days, but the time seemed to stretch on in front of her endlessly. She was sorry she'd already done the dinner dishes and finished the laundry. She needed something to do.

The ringing phone interrupted her thoughts. She walked into the kitchen and picked up the cordless telephone. When she answered and heard Ian say hello, her heart gave a little leap.

"Trish, could you go up to my office and check to make sure I unplugged the mug warmer?"

"Sure. No problem." She wished the sound of his voice didn't make her feel so wonderful. She headed toward the stairs.

There was a long pause as she waited for him to say goodbye.

"I hope the phone didn't wake Emma."

Trish laughed as she climbed to the second floor. "She's such a good sleeper, I doubt she'd wake if the phone was in her crib."

Ian chuckled. "Well, I'd better go."

She flipped on the light in his office. "Have a good flight."

"Thanks. You take care of yourself." He disconnected.

Trish pressed the off button, then held the phone against her chest. "I will, Ian. You take care, too," she whispered.

She crossed to his desk and checked the tiny hot plate he used to keep his endless cups of coffee warm while he wrote. He hadn't forgotten to unplug it.

This was the first time she'd been in his office without him here. He'd made it very clear he did not want to be interrupted as he worked, so she hadn't had an opportunity to give it a good cleaning. His work hours were erratic enough she hadn't wanted to start the job and annoy him by being in here when he was ready to start work.

She went downstairs, checked on Emma and traded the cordless phone for the crib monitor and a bucket of cleaning supplies. She cleaned every inch of his office, taking great care not to disturb the piles of papers on his desk. Then she went into his bedroom and tidied up. His bed was made, but some of his drawers were open, as if he'd scooped things out to pack and then just left. She tidied things up, then decided to shower and crawl into bed.

As she lay curled up under the cozy down comforter, she found herself thinking about Ian instead of drifting off to sleep. The big party would be tomorrow night. He'd be there with all the stars of the movie, and all the other beautiful people who attended an event like that. And Joyce.

She'd seen coverage of movie preview parties on the television shows that followed the entertainment industry. All the beautiful women in their glittering dresses and makeup and jewelry and the men in tuxedos.

Ian had taken his tuxedo. She'd seen it hanging on his closet door, still in the bag from the cleaner. She had no doubt he'd look devastating in formal evening wear. So tall and handsome, he was built to wear a suit like that.

Joyce would wear something dramatic, probably showing a lot of skin. Joyce could pull off a dress like that. Trish tried not to feel jealous, but it was a losing battle. She had to remind herself that they had a relationship, and it was none of her business.

As she drifted off to sleep, she imagined herself at the party with him. She'd wear a dress with sequins all over it so every time she moved the dress would shimmer. And high heels and sheer stockings. She'd be witty and sophisticated, and Ian would fall in love with her.

Somewhere during the dream, she heard a clock strike midnight and she found herself running down a staircase away from the party, headed for home, all alone.

Trish sighed and rolled over, snuggling under the covers. The Cinderella dream was fun, but it was only a fairy tale. And her dreams had never come true.

The telephone awakened her the next day. She jumped out of bed and shuddered as her bare feet hit the cold floor. She grabbed the telephone in the kitchen. "Hello, Blacksmith Farm."

"Trish. Did I wake you?"

How wonderful that the first thing to hear in the morning was Ian's voice.

"No." She didn't want him to think she stayed in bed and didn't do her work just because he was away. She glanced at the clock.

"Did you land already?" It was 6:30 in the morning East Coast time. That meant is was still the middle of the night in Los Angeles.

"No. We're somewhere over Nevada right now, near Las Vegas."

Trish had never flown, and the thought of hurtling through space in a huge metal object defying gravity scared her a little. "Is everything okay?"

"Sure. When the mail arrives, I need you to be on the lookout for the papers from the car dealer. I don't want them to get lost. I think I gave them my home address instead of the accountant."

"Of course." That seemed like an odd request. She sorted the mail, but always left it all for him.

There was a bit of silence. "Well, that was all. Everything okay there?"

"Everything's fine." Didn't he trust her to take care of things?

"You have my cell number if you need me for anything, right?"

"Yes, it's right here by the telephone."

"Okay. You and Emma have a good day."

"I will. Thank you."

"See you tomorrow." He hung up.

She placed the handset back on the charger. She didn't like to think of him on the airplane. It seemed impossible that someone could fly across the country and go to a party and be back in thirty-six hours.

Emma was starting to stir, so Trish got her and settled down on the couch to feed her. She switched on the news channel and caught the national weather. She already knew it was forty-five degrees at the farm and looked as if it might snow.

According to the news, in Los Angeles it was seventy-six and sunny. She wondered why Ian didn't stay for a few days.

To Trish it was a no-brainer. A few days in the sun sounded heavenly.

Today Trish was going to box up everything in the stone house so the workers could start, but first she decided to really clean Ian's room. It was easier with him out of the house. She felt a little strange going into his room when he was home.

As soon as Emma went down for her nap, Trish went upstairs. First thing, she pulled back the comforter on the huge bed to strip the sheets. Ian's male scent wafted up to her and she had the sudden urge to bury her face in the linens.

How foolish was that?

Embarrassed by her odd yearnings, she took the clothes in the hamper, rolled them up in the sheets, and heaved the bundle down the stairs.

She cleaned the room and went downstairs to check on Emma and start the laundry. She stuffed the sheets into the washer and sorted his clothes. Two of the sweaters in the hamper were dry-clean-only, so she set them aside to take into town on her next trip.

While she was feeding Emma, the phone rang again. This time she wasn't surprised to hear Ian's voice.

"Could you do me a favor?"

"Of course."

"I think my cleaning is ready today. Could you pick it up?"

She *always* picked up his cleaning. Actually it had been ready two days ago. It would have been a waste of gasoline to make a special trip to town for it. Ian had never been the least bit interested in his dry cleaning before.

"Sure. I'll get it this afternoon." In the background Trish heard Joyce's voice.

"Gotta go," he said. "See you to-morrow."

Trish disconnected and settled back with the baby. Suddenly it struck her. Ian wasn't calling because he didn't trust her to get things done. He was calling because he missed the farm. Missed being home. She liked that he thought of Blacksmith Farm as home.

A few weeks ago she was hoping he'd be an absentee owner. Now she was so glad he lived here.

And maybe, a little voice inside her said, maybe he missed her, too. But that was silly. He was in a big city with a glamorous woman, getting ready for a party that would make the top news. Why would he miss her?

In any case, she was looking forward to him coming home.

After a quick lunch, Trish bundled up Emma, grabbed Ian's two sweaters for the dry cleaners and headed into town. Her palms still became damp every time she drove the truck, but she was getting used to parking and maneuvering through town.

The first stop she made was the thrift shop. As usual, the two older ladies who ran the cash register made a fuss over Emma.

"Oh, my, she's getting so big!"

Trish laughed. "That's why we're here. She's outgrowing everything she owns!"

The ladies laughed, and the younger of the two offered to hold Emma while Trish shopped. "My daughter lives in Seattle and

I miss my grandchildren so much."

"Are you sure?" She'd gotten to know the ladies since she'd moved to the farm and she trusted them, but didn't want to impose.

"No problem. It's so quiet in here right now. If it gets busy, we'll give her back."

Trish agreed and handed the baby over to the smiling woman. It would be so much easier to shop without holding her. She headed for the children's clothes and began going through the racks. She found a snowsuit for Emma. It was a little big, but it would last all winter.

There was a pair of overalls and two little shirts that would work, too, so she brought those up to the register. She eyed a tiny pink coverall with a lace collar and pretty trim around the cuffs. Emma would look darling in it, but she put it back. Four items were enough.

The woman holding Emma had settled into a rocking chair by the cash register and was rocking the baby and singing to her. Emma seemed entranced by the sound of the lullaby.

Trish couldn't carry a tune and didn't know any lullabies. No one had ever sung to her as far as she could remember.

"Nothing for yourself?"

Trish shrugged. She didn't usually look at the women's clothes when she came in. They were usually too big, and she really needed to save her money.

The woman at the cash register took the baby clothes from Trish. "Go look. We got some extrasmalls in yesterday, and today is buy-two-items, get-one-free. You have four things here, so whatever you pick out is on the house."

Trish was tempted to go back and find something else for Emma, but the thought of something pretty for herself was too appealing.

Feeling selfish, she walked over to the racks of women's knit tops and found the extrasmall section. A light-blue sweater with a rounded neckline and soft full sleeves caught her eye. The baby-fine yarn was the color of a spring sky. Trish pulled the garment off the rack and held it out at arm's length.

It was so pretty she couldn't talk herself into putting it back. She hadn't had anything new since before she got pregnant with Emma.

She carried the sweater up to the register and laid it on top of the baby clothes.

"Did you see the pants that go with this?" The woman folded the sweater.

"They're on the rack by the coats. She pointed to a corner of the store. "Still have the tags on them."

Trish thought she'd just go and look. She found the pants right away. They were a pretty subtle plaid in a beautiful fabric that looked like wool, but the tag said machine wash. The tag also said they were her size.

She ran her hand over the fabric and wanted them. Rarely did she covet anything for herself, but she wanted this outfit. She wanted to get dressed up and look pretty.

So Ian would notice.

How silly was that?

But she took the pants off the rack and carried them to the register.

"Now you only need to pay for four."

The little pink outfit for Emma called to Trish. "Wait. I need a few more things."

Trish threw caution to the wind and went to get the pink outfit for Emma, another pair of jeans and some warm boots for herself.

If Ian ever wanted to go out to lunch again she'd have something decent to wear.

She pulled her cash from her pocket and peeled off enough bills to pay for the clothes, trying to ignore the guilt of spending money on herself.

Her job seemed fairly secure with Ian. She should be able to relax a little, but she couldn't forget she still had debts and no savings. She still owed the hospital and the funeral home and made payments to them every month.

Trish took the bag of clothes, picked Emma up out of the arms of the woman who had been holding her and headed for the dry cleaners and the grocery store, silently thanking Ian for the use of the truck. It certainly made life easier.

She glanced at the clock on the dashboard and calculated the time difference. What would Ian be doing in California right now? Probably having lunch at a really trendy restaurant, maybe a lunch meeting. Or maybe just Ian and Joyce. Trish preferred the image of him with a group of successful people who could make brilliant conversation and knew all the right things to order off the menu.

She wished she could picture herself at that table, but she knew she'd disappear with people like that. She'd just fade into nothingness.

The thought was so depressing Trish laughed at herself for even considering the possibility she would ever be included in Ian's life.

She was his housekeeper. And, she tried to convince herself, that was fine with her.

Ian made good time on the early-morning drive home from the airport in Philadelphia, despite a rainstorm. When he turned onto Blacksmith Road and caught sight of the house through the bare branches of the apple orchard, a feeling of peace descended on him.

Home.

The place really felt like home.

He pulled up by the front door, grabbed his bag and made a dash to the porch. His packing for California had not included an umbrella.

Tollie came out of the barn, barking up a frenzy. He stopped and sniffed the air and seemed to recognize Ian. The dog wagged his tail and turned and went back into the barn.

He turned the doorknob and found the door locked. Well, that was good, he thought. Trish should keep the door locked when she was here alone. He started to knock, then decided if she was busy with work or the baby, he didn't want to disturb her to answer the door.

He fished his key out of his pocket and let himself into the house. A faint odor of wood smoke and chocolate chip cookies hung in the air. He went through to the great room and glanced into the empty crib. Emma wasn't sleeping so she must be with Trish.

He thought of the fuzzy pink stuffed kitten he'd picked up at the airport for the baby. And the tiny blue T-shirt for Trish. He had an ulterior motive for the gifts. He wanted Emma to like him, and he wanted to see Trish in something other than a big flannel shirt. He had a purely male desire to know what the woman looked like under her too-big clothes.

Ian went to the bottom of the stairs and called, "Trish?"

There was no answer.

He took the stairs two at a time and called out to Trish, but he knew she wasn't in the house. It felt deserted.

Maybe she was in the barn feeding Max. Ian put his bag inside his room and came down the stairs. He grabbed a slicker from the hook by the back door. He ran down to the barn and pushed the big sliding door open. The smell of warm hay and animals greeted him, along with Tollie. Max hung his head over his stall and whinnied, and the cat, curled up on a bale of hay, stretched and pointedly ignored him.

"Trish?" he called.

No answer. Ian stood there, feeling a prickle of unease. The truck was parked beside the barn, it was raining, and she had the baby with her. Where would she go?

Maybe she was at the stone house. Work was to start on Monday, and Trish had mentioned wanting to box up things to make way.

Ian left the barn and jogged down to the old house. The rain had let up, but his shoes were a muddy mess. He opened the door to find a stack of boxes in the middle of the floor. No Trish and no Emma.

Rain was dripping from several leaks in the roof. An assortment of pans and buckets caught the drips. He closed the door, wondering how anyone could have lived there.

Ian headed back to the house. Where could they be? Could she have gone off with someone for the day? She knew he was coming in on a red-eye flight, and he was disappointed she wasn't here.

He let himself in the back door and took off his muddy shoes and dripping slicker. He supposed she had friends, but she'd never mentioned them, nor had anyone come to the house.

He found himself in the uncomfortable position of feeling jealous over someone he wasn't even sure existed.

What if something had happened to Trish, or to Emma? The thought made him feel ill. What if she had to take the baby to the doctor, or had to go herself?

The truck was there, but maybe she couldn't drive. He knew she knew the neighbors across the road, but he didn't know their name, so he couldn't call. Maybe they would know where she was.

He opened the front door and spotted Trish walking up the driveway. She had Emma buttoned inside her jacket. Her tiny head, covered by a knit cap, bobbed under Trish's chin.

The rush of relief on seeing her caught him by surprise and threw him off balance. He didn't like this feeling. He stood on the porch, his hands fisted on his hips.

Trish saw him and waved.

When she was about twenty feet away he yelled at her. "Where the hell have you been?"

She stopped midstride. "I . . . I went over to the Schmidt's to return the snake I borrowed." She started walking toward him slowly.

"Snake?" He relaxed a bit. "You borrowed a snake?"

She gave him a wary look as she came closer. "The farm doesn't have one."

They had a dog and a cat and horse. Why not a snake? "Why did you need a snake?"

Emma spotted him, blinked, then smiled. Ian felt a little warm sensation in his chest.

Trish gestured toward the house. "The drain in the downstairs bath and laundry room was stopped up."

Ian realized she was not talking about a reptile but some kind of tool. "Why didn't you call a plumber?"

"Do you know what they charge?"

"For heaven's sake, Trish, you don't have to muck out a clogged drain!"

Her shoulders got all stiff and a stubborn look crossed her face. "It's my job. And I can do it."

Ian knew when to back off. She was right, it was her job. But he had begun to forget she worked for him and had started to think of her as . . . what? He couldn't really define their relationship. When had he become so fond of her?

Feeling as if he had stepped into quicksand, he said, "I know you can do it, but you don't have to. Is there a plumber you use when something major happens?"

"Yes."

"Well, just call him when you need him."

"I can, but it usually takes him at least a day to get here, and the drain is so blocked up I couldn't do laundry. It's easier to do it myself."

He didn't know what to say without making a further fool of himself, so he let it drop, and they stood there on the front porch in awkward silence.

"Ian?" She reached out as if she was going to touch him, then drew her hand back.

"Yes?" He wished she would touch him. He wanted her to stroke his arm and caress his face and tell him he was going to be all right, because he needed to be reassured, and he didn't even know why.

She searched his face as if she was looking for the clue to this whole awkward situation. "Did you have a bad flight?"

"It was rough. I'm tired." The flight had been smooth as could be, and he had slept through the whole thing, but Trish was giving him an excuse for acting like a jerk and he wasn't going to turn it down.

Immediately her look softened and she smiled at him. "Let's go in the house and

I'll fix you some breakfast. Are you hungry?"

And just like that he felt like he was home, in a way he had never felt before.

"Sure, that would be great."

Chapter Twelve

Trish had the *New York Times* spread all over the kitchen table and was reading the reviews for the movie based on Ian's book. It had gotten two thumbs up from the critics and had broken opening-day records at the box office.

She was wearing the pretty shirt he'd brought her under her flannel shirt, and wished the weather was warm enough so she could wear it by itself.

He'd thought about her enough to bring her a gift. And one for Emma, too. To him, it was probably a little thing, but to her it was huge. She didn't get gifts.

Trish pulled her thoughts back to the paper. She couldn't believe she knew someone famous. It was thrilling to know Ian had actually met the stars in the movie.

She heard Ian coming down the stairs and jumped up to greet him. "I was just reading about your movie. It had great reviews and a huge opening weekend."

Ian stared at her. "*My* movie?"

Surely he hadn't forgotten. He'd returned yesterday from the premiere. "Yes! You wrote it."

Ian shook his head. "I wrote the book they *based* the screenplay on. Loosely."

"Is the screenplay so different from the book?"

"I don't know. They usually are. I haven't seen the movie."

What was he talking about? He went to the premiere. "Don't they show the movie at the premiere?"

"Sure. But I didn't watch it. I had dinner with some friends instead."

Trish just stared at him, trying not to think about the fact that Joyce was probably one of those friends.

How could he not watch? This was his third book that had been made into a movie. "Did you see the other two?"

He nodded. "Yes. I'll see this one eventually. Did you see the other two?"

"Sure. I thought they were good. Not as good as the books, but good."

He looked startled. "So, you read the books?"

"I've read *all* your books."

He looked pleased. "Well. Thank you."

She turned to pour him a cup of coffee. Trish wondered at his reaction. He sold millions of copies and must run into fans all the time.

He took the cup of coffee and stared at her for a moment, then said, "We should celebrate. Let's go out tonight. We can go to dinner and see the movie."

His tone was so gruff it took her a moment to realize he was asking her out.

Before she could answer, he said, "How do you think Emma would do for a couple of hours at the theater?"

The feeling of disappointment came swiftly. Emma had another cold. "Normally she'd do fine, but she has the sniffles and she's pretty fussy."

As if on cue, Emma woke up and whimpered. Trish ducked into her room and picked her up, cooing to her as she held her up against her shoulder and walked back to the great room. Emma laid her head on Trish's shoulder.

"Would you like breakfast? I made batter for waffles."

Ian studied her for a moment as he sipped his coffee. "Sounds good, but I think I'll go for a walk first. In about a half hour?"

"Sure." That would give her time to nurse Emma.

Ian put his cup in the sink and headed for the porch.

Trish got the baby back to sleep, plugged in the waffle iron and cleared the paper off the table, trying to tamp down her disappointment. She certainly would have loved to go with Ian tonight to eat and see the movie, but with Emma not feeling well, it just wasn't possible.

She lifted the first waffle out of the waffle iron and put it in the oven to keep warm. Carefully she spooned more batter into the iron, then put the butter and a pitcher of heated syrup on the table.

She set the table and as she poured a glass of orange juice, she heard him come in the front door.

He came into the room, his hair windblown and his face ruddy from the cold. "It smells fantastic in here. I'm starving."

She thought *he* looked good enough to eat. "Good walk?" she asked, wishing he wasn't so attractive. And unattainable.

"Cold, but beautiful. I love the winter landscape."

Trish found the gray landscape depressing and longed for spring. Maybe his trip to California had given him enough sun to tide him over until the trees leafed out.

He stood looking at the table and

frowned. "Have you eaten already?"

"No, not yet," she said, surprised. She always ate after he did. It was her job to wait on him.

"How come the table is only set for one?"

The table was *always* set for one. She was trying to think of an answer that wouldn't make him look silly when he said, "I want to talk to you. Sit with me."

"Okay." Instantly he'd put her on her guard.

What was this about? He always ate alone, and he didn't seem to want conversation while he did it. Often he would stand up and carry his plate upstairs or ask that his food be brought up to his office.

What did he want to talk about?

Feeling ridiculously nervous, Trish got out silverware and a plate for herself, and brought the waffles to the table. Why did he want her to sit with him?

After she sat down she remembered his coffee. She got him a fresh mug and sat again. Then she felt thirsty, so she got up for a glass of water for herself. Just as she sat down the indicator light on the waffle maker went out, so she pushed back her chair.

"Sit!" Ian made a frustrated gesture with

his hand. "You're like a jack-in-the-box."

"But the rest of the waffles are done."

He scowled at her. "Okay, but this is the last time you get up. You're going to give me indigestion."

Trish grabbed the waffle plate and added the last waffle to the stack, then returned to her seat and waited for whatever bad news Ian was about to give her.

He'd polished off three waffles and she was still chewing her first bite. She couldn't seem to swallow.

He leaned back in his chair, his thumbs hooked in his waistband. "I finished my first draft."

That didn't sound like bad news. Trish finally managed to swallow. She picked up her glass for a sip of water.

"That's good, right?" She was treading on unknown territory here. He'd never talked about his writing before.

He shrugged, looking puzzled. "It's great. I've never had a book come together like this one has."

She studied his face. "You don't look very pleased."

Ian shrugged. "I'm afraid when I start to do rewrites it will be terrible and I'll have to start over."

Trish was shocked. He'd written an entire book and didn't even know if he liked it? "Has that ever happened to you before? Having to start over, I mean?"

He thought for a moment, then shrugged. "Never."

She put her glass down. "When are you going to start the rewrite?"

"Now." He pushed his chair back and stood up.

Trish looked up at him. "How long until you know if it's good?"

Ian laughed. "I'll know right away. You're not eating."

Trish cut herself a bite of waffle. Now that she realized he wasn't bothered by something she'd done, her appetite returned with a vengeance. She raised the fork, then didn't take the bite. "Will you tell me if it's good?"

"You'll know. If I stay up there, it's going well." He walked over to the coffeemaker and poured himself another cup.

Trish put her fork on her plate. "And if it's not?"

Ian shrugged. "I don't do frustration very well. You'll hear me." He turned to leave the room.

She started to get up to clear the table.

"Please, Trish, sit down and eat."

Startled, she saw he had turned back

and was watching her. "I will. I just need to —"

"Eat. You need to eat. A nursing mother needs an extra nine hundred calories a day."

She stood there with her mouth hanging open, then snapped her jaw closed and sat when he pointed at her plate. He waited until she'd taken a bite, then turned and headed toward the stairs.

She watched him go, flabbergasted.

How did he know how many calories a nursing mother needed?

She took another bite of waffle. That wasn't the kind of information a guy could usually just pull out of his brain.

Ian stood and stretched, staring out the window, trying to make sense of what was unfolding in his writing. He'd been at the rewrites for four hours. The manuscript was better than he had dared to expect.

It felt so odd. He'd never been able to write with someone around before. Here at the farm there had been plenty of interruptions, yet everything on the first draft had gone so smoothly it was as if the book was practically writing itself and taking him along for the ride.

He really wanted to go out and celebrate, but he understood why Trish couldn't take Emma. People who paid for a movie ticket didn't want to try to hear dialogue over the sounds of a fussy baby.

In the distance he saw the school bus pull up on the main road. The two children who lived at the farm across the fields got out. One was a boy who looked to be about ten, and the other was a teenage girl.

Girls that age baby-sat, didn't they? Maybe he could talk Trish into leaving Emma with a baby-sitter.

He needed to check the girl out first, before he even made the suggestion. If she had a ring in her nose and wore black lipstick, the deal would be off.

Ian went downstairs. He heard Trish in the laundry room talking to the baby. Wanting the evening out to be a surprise, he didn't mention where he was going. He went through the great room to the side porch, grabbed his jacket, changed into a pair of rubber boots and went out.

Tollie was asleep in the sun on the steps. He jumped up when Ian opened the door and followed him companionably down the driveway.

When Ian cut across the barren muddy field, the dog turned back toward the house. Ian walked to the road, then crossed over to the neighboring property.

Behind the fence was a herd of about fifteen miniature ponies. They saw him coming and ran back up toward the barn, then turned and stared at him and whinnied. Their comical behavior made him smile.

Ian turned up the driveway toward a newer wood frame house. The door opened and a middle-aged woman in an apron stepped out onto the porch as he approached. The noise the little animals were making must have alerted her to his arrival.

She smiled at him tentatively. "May I help you?"

Ian introduced himself, and the woman told him her name was Ellen Schmidt and welcomed him to the neighborhood.

"I was wondering if your daughter did baby-sitting?"

She gave him a speculative look. "She does. For the Jenecks down the road. They have five children." The woman sounded proud of her daughter.

"How old is she?" Ian wasn't sure how old a babysitter should be.

"Sarah is fifteen, but she is very mature and dependable."

"Then taking care of Emma should be a

snap. May I speak to her?" he asked, smiling at Ellen's pride in her daughter.

"Sure. She's in the barn feeding the ponies." She stepped off the porch and headed to the barn with Ian following.

Ian looked around and noticed the little creatures were nowhere in sight. He followed her through the gate.

She called into the big open doors. "Sarah? Come out for a minute."

Ian heard a muffled reply and in a moment a brunette teenager emerged from the barn. As far as Ian could tell she didn't even have pierced ears, and wore no makeup.

"Sarah, this is Ian Miller. He lives across the road in the plank house. He's interested in hiring you to baby-sit for Emma."

Sarah smiled shyly. "Trish's baby? Sure."

Ian studied the teenager, as if he could discern her character. "Are you free tonight?"

"Yes."

Ian turned to Sarah's mother. "Will you be home? In case your daughter needs help?"

The woman nodded, looking amused. "My husband and I will be here."

"Now I just have to convince Trish to leave Emma at home."

The woman smiled. "Good luck. Trish is very protective. Maybe if Sarah comes over after she finishes her chores and Trish talks to her she'll feel better about it."

"Good idea," Ian agreed, and headed home.

When he walked in the porch door, he was greeted by a wide-eyed Trish holding Emma. "The delivery service just left. I signed for you."

He'd been expecting the galleys of his next book. "Did you put it in my office?"

Trish shook her head and smiled. "I don't think it would fit."

She gestured toward the front room. He walked down the short hallway and stopped in the doorway. There was an enormous basket of fruit wrapped in cellophane, three flower arrangements and two huge boxes.

Ian inspected the labels on the boxes and basket, then pulled the cards out of the flowers and read them. The gifts were from his agent, his publisher, the movie studio and his brother-in-law, who kept pestering him to coproduce his next movie. "Seems like everyone is pleased with the movie's success."

Trish smiled. "It looks that way. Do they always do this?"

"To a point. The deal this time cut everyone in on profits instead of a flat upfront fee, so they'll make a lot more if it's a success."

Trish grinned. "I read the papers. It's already a success." Then her expression sobered. "You went out for a walk. Did you need to find a place to let out your frustration?"

For a moment he didn't know what she was talking about, then he remembered the comment about the rewrites he'd made earlier.

He was touched that she'd remembered. "Actually, the book is going better than I expected. I walked across the road to see if Sarah could baby-sit tonight, so you and I can go celebrate." He watched for her reaction.

Trish stared at him and he could see her tighten her grip on Emma. "I don't know — I, uh, I've never left her."

Ian was shocked. "Never?"

"No. She's only three and a half months old," she said defensively.

Ian remembered his mother proudly telling the story of how she'd managed to get her figure back so quickly that when he was two weeks old she could fit into her ski clothes. She'd left him with his nurse and

180

gone off for a two-week ski trip. But then, he thought wryly, his mother had never been the dedicated mother Trish was.

He was about to argue his case when the doorbell rang.

"I hope that isn't another fruit basket," Trish muttered as she went for the door.

Sarah was standing on the porch, and Trish let her in. Ian stood back and watched the interaction between the two females as they cooed and fussed over Emma.

He decided to go upstairs and let them work it out. He wanted to go and celebrate, but he didn't want to pressure Trish into something that would make her uncomfortable. He didn't understand her reluctance to leave the baby, but it was her choice.

He was searching through a reference book when she knocked on his doorframe.

"Sarah's free tonight. Is the offer to see your movie still open?"

Ian didn't want to examine the rush of pleasure he felt too closely. After all, they were just going to a movie.

"Sure. I'll see what time the show is playing." He moved to his computer and did a quick search for the theater.

She nodded, and seemed suddenly shy

and tentative. "Okay. Let me know what time you want to leave. I can fix an early dinner."

He shook his head. "No, let's go out. Call it your night off." She never took a day off and she'd certainly earned it. "Have Sarah come back at 6:00. That will give us time to eat first."

He keyed in the strokes necessary to purchase the tickets online.

When he looked up, he was disappointed to see she was gone.

Trish felt a curious mixture of excitement and guilt. She wanted to go out with Ian and see his movie in the worst way, but she had never left Emma before.

Emma sat in her infant seat on the dresser and grabbed for the string of toys that dangled in front of her. Trish leaned over, wiped her little runny nose and caught the baby's gaze. "You know how much I love you, don't you?"

Emma kicked her feet and gurgled a reply, then sneezed. Trish felt her forehead. The baby's skin was cool to the touch.

Trish took her new sweater and slacks from the closet and laid them on the bed, smoothing the fabric with her hand. She knew Sarah had experience with babies, and Sarah had assured her her mother would be home tonight, but Trish had never been away from her baby.

She carried Emma, seat and all, into the bathroom and set her on the floor. Then she peeled off her clothes and stepped into the shower. As the hot water beat down on her head, she knew she had to leave Emma with someone else sooner or later, but her own issues with abandonment made it hard.

She worked to convince herself it would be all right. Ian had a cell phone so she could check on Emma, and Sarah could call if there were any problem.

Trish worked the shampoo into her hair and stepped back under the spray. She could nurse Emma and put her to bed a little early and Emma would never know she was gone.

She turned off the water, stepped out of the shower and dried off. Feeling giddy with excitement she glanced at her reflection in the foggy mirror and said, "You're going out tonight with one of Philadelphia's most eligible bachelors." A magazine article the month before had named him to the list.

Of course, the only reason he'd asked her was because he wanted to celebrate.

She was the only one he knew for sixty miles, but he *had* asked *her.*

Her, Trish Ryan, a little nobody who had just happened to end up being a house-keeper for one of the most gorgeous men on the planet. She'd never had good luck, but recently things had begun to look up.

Trish wrapped herself in her robe and settled down on her bed to nurse her baby.

"Mommy's only leaving for a few hours. You know that, don't you, baby girl?" She stroked Emma's fine baby hair. "I'll be home to feed you. I'll never leave you, never."

She didn't know it was possible to feel this much emotion for another living being and wondered why her own mother had abandoned her. What had happened? What had Trish done that was so bad her mother would leave her at a gas station in the middle of the night and never come back for her?

She shoved the dark thoughts away as she put the sleeping baby in her crib and got dressed.

There were no answers, and there never would be. Tonight she wasn't going to dwell on dark thoughts. Tonight she was going out to dinner and a movie with Ian Miller.

Trish slid her new sweater over her head, so glad she had decided to splurge. The knit was soft and smelled sweet after she had so carefully washed it. She fluffed her hair by running her fingers through it. There wasn't much more she could do. Her hair was so curly, it would take an hour with a blow-dryer to tame it down, and she didn't have the time, equipment or expertise.

She stepped into the slacks, pulled them up and fastened them, brushing her hand over the fine fabric. It was the nicest outfit she'd ever owned. She slipped her feet into her one pair of decent leather shoes, hand-me-down loafers from high school that were still in pretty good shape.

Just as she finished dressing, she heard the doorbell ring. She grabbed her jacket off the end of the bed and hurried.

Ian had beaten her to the door. She stopped and watched as he ushered Sarah into the front room.

He was smiling and talking to the teenager, who was gazing at him with an adoring look. She recognized the look and imagined most women felt that way when they came face-to-face with a man who looked like Ian.

Before Trish could say a word, he

handed Sarah a written list of where they would be and his cell number. If she wasn't already in love with him, she'd have fallen right then.

Ian turned and saw her and faltered for a moment. It was so unlike him to look uncertain she immediately wondered what was wrong.

Was it her clothes? Had she gotten too dressed up? Would he think she was trying too hard to impress him? Trish was sure women did that all the time. She didn't want him to think that was what she was doing. She never wanted him to know how she felt about him. It would be too embarrassing.

Then he smiled and waved her over. She was overreacting, she thought with a little spurt of relief. He'd dressed up, too. He'd shaved and showered and changed into slacks, a knit shirt and a handsome leather jacket.

Trish greeted Sarah and gave her some last-minute instructions and showed her where the crib was, the remote for the TV, the cordless telephone and the bottle of breast milk she'd pumped earlier, just in case Emma woke up before Trish got home.

When Trish wound down, Ian waited for

a moment, then touched her elbow. "I think you have it covered." He took her jacket and held it for her as she slipped her arms into the sleeves.

Trish nodded, suddenly wanting to call the evening off and stay home. She fought off the urge to go back to the crib and take a last look at the peacefully sleeping baby.

Instead she screwed up her courage and faced Ian. "I'm ready."

Ian shook his head. "You're going to a movie, not an execution."

Trish tried to smile. He couldn't understand how she felt, and there was no way to explain it.

The last thing Ian said to Sarah as they went through the door was, "Eat whatever you want."

Sarah waved and closed the door.

They were alone. Suddenly nervous, Trish headed for the truck.

"Whoa. Over this way. We'll take the car." He opened the passenger door of his low-slung black sports car. She slid onto the leather seat and sank into the plush interior.

He settled himself in the driver's seat and turned the key. The engine grumbled then sprang to life with a deep roar.

Trish glanced around at the leather interior and the smooth wood on the dashboard. She'd never been in a car like this before, and she resisted the urge to run her hands over the fine wood.

He fiddled with the heater, then pulled out of the parking area beside the barn and headed down the gravel drive, the headlights sweeping over the still-bare branches of the trees across the fallow field. She could feel the power of the car vibrating through the seats.

"How long until Emma needs to eat?" he asked as he expertly shifted gears.

Trish turned to look at his strong profile highlighted in the glowing lights on the dashboard. "She usually sleeps until I wake her to feed her right before I go to bed. Around eleven."

"Good. Then we have plenty of time for dinner and the movie. Can you handle it? Being away that long?"

"Is it okay if I use your phone and call in about an hour?"

He turned and looked at her. "You can call as often as you need to."

She cleared her throat. "Thanks for understanding."

He studied her for a moment. "I don't. Not really. But that's not the important thing, is it?"

With those few words, she fell even more in love with him. Who could resist a man like Ian?

He turned onto the highway and they flew along in silence. She was comfortable not talking, and so was he apparently, so she decided to try not to think too much about Emma and Sarah and to just enjoy the thrill of the ride and being with him.

He pulled up in front of a restaurant with an Italian name, and he glanced over at her. "Do you like Italian?"

She liked anything she didn't have to cook, and Italian was at the top of her list. "Yes."

Suddenly her door opened, startling her. A young man in a white shirt and black jacket held the door for her. "Ma'am?"

He held out his hand and she realized he must think she needed help getting out of the car the way she was sitting there. She ignored his hand and scrambled out.

Ian stood on the curb waiting for her. As she came around the side of the car he tossed the keys to the young man.

Amazed, she just stared at Ian, then at the young man sliding into the seat of the car. Finally Ian took her arm and gave her a gentle tug to get her started.

As she watched the car turn the corner,

she said, "You're going to trust him with your car? You don't even know him."

Ian smiled. "It's his job to park cars for the restaurant. What, you think he's going to drive off and we'll never see him again?"

Trish felt foolish, but then she'd known a few guys who would have chucked a minimum-wage job in favor of stealing an expensive sports car.

Ian chuckled. "If he doesn't come back, we'll call a cab to get to the theater."

On edge, Trish glanced up at him. She was feeling off balance and out of place. "Don't laugh at me."

Immediately he sobered. "I wasn't. I just don't want you to worry about anything. You deserve to have a nice evening."

Trish felt foolish and didn't answer as they stepped into the plush interior of the restaurant. It smelled of garlic and cheese and fresh bread.

The hostess showed them to a table next to a window, and Ian pulled her chair out for her. There were linen napkins and wineglasses on the table. The hostess handed them the menus and left, telling them their waiter would be right with them.

Trish opened the menu and tried not to look at the prices. If she was paying, this meal would cost her half a week's salary. She had a sudden panicky thought. Ian would insist on paying, wouldn't he? He had invited her.

"What looks good?" his voice interrupted her thoughts.

She peered at him over the top of the menu and answered truthfully. "Everything!" She couldn't pronounce the names of the dishes, but the descriptions sounded heavenly.

He glanced back at his menu. "Do you want me to order for you?"

She hesitated for a moment, then decided she'd enjoy the food more if she didn't know what it cost. "Okay."

The waiter appeared and Ian ordered wine, which she refused, and a sparkling water for her.

"Would it be okay for me to call Sarah? I won't talk very long."

"Sure." He opened the little fold-up phone and handed it to her.

She'd never used a cell phone before. She stared at it for a moment, and he said, "Just punch in the number and hit the green send button."

Sarah answered on the first ring and assured Trish that Emma was sleeping and all was well. Trish thanked her and hung up.

When the man returned with a glass of wine on a silver tray, Ian rattled off their food order in Italian. The man smiled and said their salads would be right up.

She was impressed. "Do you speak Italian?"

"Enough to order food. I spent a summer there in college. I was supposed to be studying the language, but I got side-tracked."

Trish could imagine. She was sure the Italian women probably found him every bit as exciting as American women did.

The salads came, and as she concentrated on the wonderful greens, he entertained her with a story about a monastery near Palermo.

She had never been anywhere until she'd come here, to this town an hour out of Philadelphia.

What would it be like, to travel to Europe? To walk through the historic places she'd only read about?

"Trish." Ian's voice jerked her back. She could feel her cheeks heat as she realized while she'd been daydreaming, their waiter was standing beside her.

"Are you finished, miss?"

Trish looked down at her plate. The only thing on it was the name of the restaurant glazed into the finish. "Yes."

He took the plate and left. Ian studied her for a moment over the rim of his glass. "Are you still worried about leaving Emma?"

Trish realized she was much more comfortable than she'd expected to be. "No, not really. Sarah is experienced with children, and she can call if there's a problem."

"Good. Because I want you to come to the launch party for my new book in two weeks. It's a February release and the publisher wants to generate some publicity."

It took her a moment for his invitation to register. Wow. He was making plans ahead. "Where is it going to be?"

He leaned back in his chair. "New York."

Oh, how she wanted to say yes. New York. Just the name of the city gave her goose bumps.

She fought back her disappointment. She had to be realistic. "I can't leave Emma to go all the way to New York. We'd be gone for hours."

Ian shook his head. "Days. We'll take Emma with us. And Sarah, if it's okay with her mother. She can stay in the hotel room with Emma while we go to the party."

New York. He wanted to take her to

New York. To stay in a hotel. She was speechless.

The waiter arrived with their meal and set her plate down in front of her.

He picked up his fork and acted as if it were no big deal. "What do you say? Will you go?"

"Who will take care of the farm?" She meant the animals, but she didn't want to mention them specifically, because she knew how he felt about them.

"It will only be for a couple of days. We can ask Sarah. She must know someone in school who can stop in and feed all your critters."

Trish nodded, still stunned by his invitation. New York. Wow.

"Well?" Ian tapped his fingers on the table beside his plate and looked impatient.

She nodded, her hands gripped together in her lap. "I'd really like to go." Oh, if he only knew how much she wanted to go!

He smiled. "Good," he said casually, as if her answer one way or the other wasn't really important. "Now, please eat."

The food was wonderful. They ate in a comfortable silence, and she thought about his invitation.

She didn't care how casual he was. She

felt as if she was Cinderella and Prince Charming had just handed her an invitation to the ball.

The waiter came and cleared their plates. "May I interest you in dessert?"

Trish shook her head, but Ian said, "Do you have any chocolate *cannolis?*"

The waiter nodded.

Ian looked at Trish. "Are you sure you don't want dessert?"

She rubbed her hand over her stomach. "I can't. Too full."

Ian nodded to the waiter, and he hurried off. "We can go into the city on Friday and come home Sunday. It shouldn't be too hard to find someone over a weekend to come in a couple of times a day. Right?"

Trish felt as if she was going to explode from excitement. She took a deep breath and shook her head. "I'll ask Sarah tonight."

Ian paid the bill. She wanted to ask him all kinds of questions about the party, but didn't want him to know how naive she was about things like that.

The rest of the evening passed like a dream. She enjoyed the movie, despite Ian's occasional mutterings. Sitting beside him in the dark, she could feel his warmth and smell his aftershave.

Her attention wandered from the film. She wanted him to hold her hand, to put his arm around her. To kiss her.

She sighed. She'd always been such a dreamer.

On the way out of the theater she said, "You didn't like it?"

He shrugged. "I sold it to Hollywood. They make it into what they think they can sell."

She looked up at him as they walked to his car. "It wasn't as good as the book."

He nodded. "I know."

What would it be like to be so confident, she wondered, as he opened the car door for her. She slid into the leather seat.

As he started toward the farm a thought occurred to her. What would she wear to the party? How dressy would it be? She had her best outfit on, and she was sure the party would be dressier than slacks and a sweater.

"Is anything wrong?" Ian's voice cut into her thoughts.

She felt silly. "No. Well, yes. Not wrong, exactly."

He turned his head, raised one eyebrow and gave her an exasperated look. "What?"

"I don't know what to wear. To the party."

He shrugged as if it were unimportant. "A cocktail dress will be fine."

She smiled and nodded. Sure, a cocktail dress was fine. If you had one. When she went into town for groceries she'd have to check the thrift shop.

A cocktail dress would be a huge splurge for her budget, but she wasn't going to miss a party in New York because she didn't have a dress, and since she doubted she could count on a fairy godmother showing up, she'd visit the thrift shop.

Chapter Thirteen

Trish stood staring at the open suitcase on her bed. She'd found it stored in the basement, left behind by the previous owners. She'd scrubbed the lining twice, then aired it to get rid of the musty smell.

She'd been awake for most of the previous night. Why had she thought going to New York was a good idea?

She didn't belong in New York. The party would be full of smart, sophisticated people. She didn't belong there. Ian had been kind to invite her, but she knew he would compare her to his friends and see how lacking she really was.

If not for Sarah, Trish would back out right now. Sarah had come over for the past three days bubbling over with excitement.

With Emma cradled in one arm, Trish awkwardly folded the blue dress she'd found at the thrift shop and placed it on top of her other clothes.

Emma was unusually fussy this morning. She seemed to be picking up on Trish's growing panic.

Trish smoothed the shiny fabric. The dress was a little big, but it had matching shoes, so she'd bought it at the thrift shop to wear to the party. She had on her new sweater and slacks. That about completed her wardrobe for New York.

There was plenty of room for the small pile of Emma's clothes and her blanket. Trish had also splurged on disposable diapers. There was no way she could take cloth diapers along on the trip.

She heard Sarah coming up the stairs. "Trish! Trish!"

The teenager, face flushed, stood in the doorway.

"What's the matter?" She hoped Sarah was going to tell her she couldn't go. It would be an easy excuse for Trish to back out.

"Nothing! Did you see the car?" she asked in a rush.

"Car?" Trish hadn't heard a car arrive.

Sarah was fairly dancing. "Limousine. Outside. We're going in a limousine."

Trish walked over and looked out the window. Indeed, there was a black limousine in the circular drive.

Sarah came to stand beside Trish. "I suppose we are," Trish said, feeling faintly ill.

It only made sense, Trish thought as she handed Emma over to Sarah. They wouldn't all fit comfortably in the truck. She'd been so rattled over the trip she hadn't thought about how they would get there.

"The driver is wearing a uniform. And one of those caps. His name is Freddy and he took my suitcase and put it in the trunk."

The girl looked as if she might explode with excitement. Trish wished she felt some of it herself. Instead all she felt was dread.

"Sarah."

"What?"

"Take a breath."

Sarah giggled and spun in a circle. "I'll take Emma out to look at the car so you can finish packing." Sarah picked up Emma's tiny jacket and hat, then took the baby.

Trish forced a smile for the teenager and nodded. She *was* finished. Everything she owned except her barn clothes was in the suitcase.

Sarah left with Emma, and Trish loaded the clothes and diapers on top of her dress and closed the lid.

She turned when she heard a soft rapping on the door frame.

Ian stood there, dressed in black trousers and a black sweater. *He* looked as if he belonged in a limousine.

"You ready?" he asked with the smile that made her stomach flutter. He'd been smiling more lately, and it made him very hard to resist.

She hesitated. "Yes."

"What's the matter?"

The feelings of inadequacy that had been building came bubbling up and she blurted, "I don't think I can go."

His smile disappeared. "Why not?"

"There are things to do here. And the animals —"

He cut her off with an impatient wave of his hand. "We've been over this. What's the real reason you don't want to go?"

"Oh, Ian, I don't belong in a limousine," she wailed.

He laughed, which made her mad. He didn't understand, and she didn't know how to tell him.

"It's just a car. How does it matter how we get there?"

He was wrong. It was so much more than just the car, but he wouldn't understand. Ian was used to a life that would include a limousine.

He came into the room and picked up

her suitcase. "Is this it? Just this bag?"

Trish nodded.

He motioned to her. "Come on, then. Sarah is going to keel over from too much excitement if we don't get going."

She nodded, not feeling the least bit re-assured. "Okay. I'm ready."

How could she explain it to him? He lived in a different world. He'd probably never felt out of place in his entire life.

He smiled down at her. "Trish, cheer up. I promise this will not hurt."

She hoped he was right, but was not very confident.

Ian lifted her bag off the bed and ush-ered her to go ahead. When they passed the stairs, she had the ridiculous urge to grab the banister and hold on. Instead she rubbed her sweaty palms on her slacks and marched out to the car.

She couldn't explain her fear to him, so she'd keep it to herself.

The driver hopped out of the car and opened the door for her with a flourish. She climbed inside and saw Sarah and Emma already settled in.

"Look at this. There's a television," Sarah said in a loud whisper as she pointed to a screen in the corner, her face glowing with excitement.

Trish took in the interior of the big black car. Seats ran the length of the car instead of side to side.

She wished she could share Sarah's obvious excitement. "Pretty cool."

Sarah nodded so hard her hair bounced around her face. "I just wish all the kids at school could see this."

Sarah was missing a day of school to go with them. Trish smiled as Ian climbed in behind her. The usually quiet teenager was vibrating with excitement.

Trish slid into a place beside Emma, checked to make sure the baby's car seat was securely fastened, then fastened her own seat belt.

Ian cleared his throat. "Sarah, didn't you forget to get a book out of your locker at school? Something you'll need over the weekend?"

Sarah gave him a blank look, then a big smile spread across her face. "Do you mind making a stop?"

"We're in no hurry." Ian signaled the driver and gave him directions to the high school.

When they pulled up alongside the brick building, there were students all over the sidewalk. Everyone stopped to look at the limousine.

"Lunch?" Ian asked as he looked out the window.

Sarah swallowed and nodded. "Just started."

The driver got out and opened the door for Sarah, who scrambled over Trish. "It will only take me five minutes."

Ian smiled at her. "Take your time."

When the girl was out of the car, Trish looked over at Ian. "You made her day."

He shrugged. "I remember high school. Can't hurt to add to your 'rep.'"

Trish studied the man. She'd bet her new blue dress he'd been the coolest boy in his class.

Sarah came out of the building accompanied by several other students. She waved to them and climbed back in the car.

When the door closed she announced, "This is the best day of my life!"

Ian and Trish both laughed as the driver pulled away from the curb.

Trish only hoped it wouldn't be her own worst day.

Ian watched Trish as they headed into the city. He could tell she was nervous about the trip, but he wasn't sure what to do about it. He wanted her to have a great time.

The closer they got to the city, the quieter both Trish and Sarah got. He tried to imagine what it would be like coming into New York City for the first time. He'd been doing it since he was a child.

The driver pulled up in front of the Plaza Hotel. He jumped out and held the door.

Ian was the first one out of the passenger compartment. Trish unbuckled Emma from her car seat, and she and Sarah followed him out.

He ushered them through the door into the lobby. The hotel manager crossed the huge expanse of marble floor and greeted Ian.

"So pleased to have you back for another visit, Mr. Miller."

Ian noticed he smiled and nodded at Trish and Sarah, who stood gaping at the lobby. He'd stopped noticing years ago, but he had to admit the coffered ceilings, gilt woodwork and crystal chandeliers were impressive.

The Plaza could be counted on to be discreet, he thought wryly as he turned his attention back to the man standing in front of him. The manager would act as if Ian always arrived with a young woman, a baby and a teenager in tow.

"Your rooms are ready. If there is anything I can do to make your stay more comfortable, just let me know. James will take you up." A bellman, who had been standing a short distance away approached and motioned them to follow him.

Ian thanked the hotel manager, then herded Trish and Sarah, who seemed incapable of speech, into the elevator.

The bellman unlocked the door to the first suite and ushered them inside. Their suitcases were already upstairs. Ian was pleased to see the crib was in place and made up.

The bellman then unlocked the adjoining door to the second suite and handed Ian both the keys. "Would you like me to send a maid up to help you unpack?"

Ian glanced at Trish and Sarah, who still appeared to be in shock as they stared at the brocade bedspreads and marble fireplace, and shook his head.

He eyed Trish. He'd bet she wouldn't want someone to empty her suitcase for her. "We can manage. But I will need some pressing done. Send someone up for that, will you?"

James nodded and accepted his tip, then slipped out the door.

"Trish? Sarah?" They turned to him as if in a daze. "Shall we unpack now? Then we can go sight-seeing." He picked up his bag.

Both Sarah and Trish nodded but didn't move. "Fifteen minutes?" he asked as he headed for the adjoining door. "Trish?"

Mutely they nodded again. He went into his room and closed the door behind him, hoping the message had gotten through.

He put his clothes away and hung his tux and a pair of slacks and a shirt on the outside of the closet for the valet. He wanted to show Trish the sights, which was odd, because he generally refused to go to crowded public places.

As he looked at his remaining clothes to see if anything else needed attention, he had a thought. If Trish's dress was smashed into her suitcase, it would need pressing, too.

He couldn't believe she had packed everything for herself and the baby in one small suitcase. Most women would need two big bags for a weekend like this, just for themselves.

He moved to the adjoining door and knocked. Sarah opened the door.

Ian looked around the suite. "Where's Trish?"

Sarah blushed and pointed to the closed bathroom door.

"Did she unpack her dress? I'll send it down to get it pressed."

"It's right here." Sarah opened the closet and pulled out the ugliest electric-blue bridesmaid's dress Ian had ever seen. She must have been in someone's wedding. Someone with atrocious taste.

Ian took the dress and headed back to his suite, trying to decide what to do. After all, it was Trish's dress. Did he have the right to overrule her choice? He had to, he told himself. He suspected she'd never been to a party like the one tomorrow night, and he wanted her to have a good time. He knew how the other women would be dressed, and he didn't want her to feel self-conscious.

Ian hung the dress beside his tux and went back and knocked on the adjoining door. Sarah answered and he saw Trish sitting in an armchair by the window, nursing Emma.

"How about lunch and some sight-seeing?"

"Yes!" Both women answered in unison.

He glanced over at Trish. "How long until you can be ready?"

"Ten minutes."

"I'll be back to collect you."

The woman from valet services knocked on his door, then waited while he retrieved his things and Trish's dress. He handed the clothes over along with a large bill.

"I want this dress to disappear. Put it in a bag and hang it down in your department until you hear from me. If Ms. Ryan calls looking for it, you can't find it. Understand?"

He would not let Trish be embarrassed by wearing that dress tomorrow night, but he knew she'd be too proud to accept a replacement unless it was an emergency.

The woman looked at the dress, then at Ian, and a look of understanding spread over her face. She nodded and smiled. "Yes, sir."

Ian closed the outside door to his suite and immediately got on the phone to the manager's office. "I need to speak to a female employee, someone with a sense of style."

The manager put his assistant on the phone, and Ian asked her to make appointments at a salon for hair and nails tomorrow afternoon, then asked for the name of a shop that was appropriate for someone Trish's age and would have a range of clothes from casual to dressy.

The assistant manager said she would make all the arrangements, and hung up. Ian hoped he had made the right decision. It was the only way he could think to handle the situation without hurting Trish's feelings.

They spent the afternoon seeing the Empire State Building, Times Square and Central Park. By the time they returned to the hotel, everyone looked exhausted.

"I have that dinner meeting with my publisher. Do you want to just order room service and stay in?"

Trish covered a yawn. "I think that's a great idea."

Ian knew if Trish saw the prices for room service she wouldn't enjoy the meal. "How about I order?"

He picked up the menu and read out the offerings. Both Trish and Sarah announced they wanted hamburgers and fries. Ian placed the order, thinking he would rather stay in and eat burgers with them than go to the upscale restaurant where he was meeting his publisher. But business was business. He didn't like that part of his writing career, but it was a necessary evil.

"If you need anything, the numbers are on this directory by the telephone. I'll have my cell on so you can call me anytime." He picked up the remote control and flipped on the TV, scrolling until he got to the list of in-house movies. "Watch a movie. What do you want to see?"

They both agreed on a romantic comedy. As he ordered the movie for them he shook his head in mock dismay and said, "Chick flick."

"You bet," Trish returned with a laugh.

He'd like nothing better than to curl up on the bed with her and watch the movie. He handed her the remote and reluctantly returned to his room to get ready for his dinner.

When he returned from dinner, Ian noticed there was no light showing under the door that joined the two suites. He tried the knob and found it unlocked. He knew he should stay where he was, but he had the strange need to check on her.

Feeling like an intruder, he eased the door open and stood until his eyes became accustomed to the dark. He walked over toward the beds and recognized Trish by the halo of blond curls on the pillow. She was curled up like a child, with one hand tucked under her chin.

Without thinking about what he was doing, he bent over and kissed her gently on the temple. She muttered something in her sleep and curled into a tighter ball.

He pulled the covers up over her shoulder and checked on Emma. The baby was sleeping flat on her back, her arms thrown wide. He covered her with her blanket and slipped back into his suite.

Ian went to bed and lay awake for a long time, thinking about how his life had changed since he'd moved to the farm. He loved the house and the isolation, but the reason it all worked was Trish.

He had feelings for her he'd never had for another woman, and it scared him. As he drifted off to sleep he realized he needed her. He'd never needed anyone before, had always prided himself on his independence.

He woke up thinking the same thoughts. As he lay in the big bed, he thought about what he wanted. He wanted Trish there, beside him, not a room away. He wanted to hold her and make love to her and keep her safe. He wanted to keep the fear and worry out of her eyes. He knew that most of the worry was for her daughter.

He sat up suddenly, knowing what would make things right for Trish. He could give her security. Something she'd never had. He could set up a fund for Emma, money

Trish could draw on if she ever needed it. Would she accept it? He thought she wouldn't at first, but if it was for Emma, he might be able to convince her.

He flopped back against the pillows. Yes, he could set up a fund, but was that what he wanted?

Deep down did he want to be just financially responsible? Then another thought hit him and had him sitting up again.

He could marry her and adopt Emma. A month ago the thought of marriage and a child would have terrified him. Now it sounded right.

He tried the idea on, gave it some serious consideration. It felt right, it was practical, efficient and sensible. It would be the best situation, for Trish and for Emma. And for him.

He jumped out of bed and headed for the bathroom, his mind churning with plans.

He took a shower and dressed and had no second thoughts. The only other time he had made such a big decision so easily and felt so good about it was when he'd decided to leave the family business and devote himself to writing full-time.

There was a knock on his door. When he answered, it was the valet with his clothes.

He tipped the man and hung his things in his closet, then knocked on the adjoining door and found Trish and Sarah and Emma up and ready for the day.

"Ready for breakfast?" He noted she was dressed in the same slacks and sweater she'd worn yesterday.

"Starving!" They said in unison, then laughed.

He held out a hand toward Trish. "Before we go down to the dining room, I have some bad news. The hotel lost your dress."

Trish looked blank for a moment. "It's in the closet."

Ian shook his head. "I sent it down to be pressed."

She struggled to hide her disappointment, then said, "They'll find it." She brightened a bit. "Or I won't be able to go tonight."

He didn't like the idea that not going to the party appeared to appeal to her. "I'm taking you shopping after breakfast. Sarah can stay with Emma."

"But —"

"Trish, we're going. It was my idea to send your dress out, and I'm going to see you get a new one. The hotel will be responsible." He crossed his fingers behind his back.

She opened her mouth to complain and he cut her off. "No arguments."

She bit at her lower lip, and he could almost see the wheels turning in her head. Finally she said, "Okay. After breakfast."

Ian hid a smile. She looked like someone facing a trip to the dentist instead of shopping. Not your typical woman, he thought, and admired her even more for it.

He was going to enjoy spoiling her.

Trish looked at the dresses the salesclerk was busy collecting, wanting very badly to take a peek at the price tags, but she knew Ian was watching.

He'd been acting very strangely and she didn't know what to make of it. He kept smiling at her, and on the way to the shop he'd held her hand. He probably just didn't want her to get trampled on the busy sidewalk, but she had loved the feel of his palm against hers.

Maybe he was in such a good mood because he was in New York. She hadn't considered that he must miss the city life. Would he think the farm was boring after a weekend here?

She looked around. The store he'd brought her to was plush and beautiful. It even smelled expensive. She'd look at the tags in the dressing room when he couldn't see.

"Trish?"

She glanced up at him. "What?"

He pointed to the clerk, who stood waiting for her. Embarrassed that she'd been caught daydreaming, she followed the elegant older saleswoman into a luxurious dressing room that was larger than her bedroom. It was all done up in peach and blue and even had a couch in it. I could live here, Trish thought, and stifled a nervous laugh.

The woman hung the dresses on a rack and turned to eye Trish. She tried very hard not to squirm under her scrutiny.

"I'll be back with some undergarments." She left the room.

Keeping an eye on the door, Trish edged toward the rack and looked at the dresses. Two of them were so low cut she didn't see how anyone could fit an undergarment under them.

There were at least two tags on each dress, but unless the prices were in some kind of code, she couldn't tell how much they cost.

Trish peeled off her slacks and sweater and chose a blue dress. It would go with the shoes she already had. As she stepped into the dress and pulled it up over her hips a brisk knock sounded on the door and, before she could respond, the clerk came in.

She eyed her for a minute and said, "Not that one. The color is no good for you." She handed Trish a lacy strapless bra.

The dress was blue, and she liked it, but she wasn't going to argue with someone who considered herself an expert. She peeled off the dress and reached for the hanger. The clerk took the hanger and the dress and quickly returned it to the rack while Trish struggled with the bra. The clerk spun her around and expertly did up the hooks.

Trish eyed herself in the mirror, unsure of how she felt about all her exposed skin. Between the nursing and the undergarment, she actually had quite a bit of cleavage.

Before she could decide if she wanted to show off that much of her chest, the clerk held out a pink dress that shimmered in the light. Transfixed by the beautiful piece of clothing, Trish held up her arms, and the saleslady lifted the garment over her head. The fabric, shot through with gold flecks, slid down over Trish's hips like a silky flow of water. The skirt had a flare at the hem and ended above her knees.

"This is the one," the salesclerk announced.

Trish stared at herself in the mirror, mesmerized. Rarely did she covet things, but she wanted this dress.

She stared at her image for a moment before her practical side caught up with her.

She worked up her courage. "How much?" she asked as she shimmied out of the dress.

The clerk took the dress and shrugged. "That's not important. The important thing is that it's right for you. Most of the women at the party will be wearing black. Black is not for you. You'll stand out in this."

She asked her shoe size and left the room, dress in hand, before Trish could insist she tell her the price.

Trish struggled out of the undergarment and pulled her clothes on. Did she want to stand out? Not really. Her goal was to get through the evening without anyone noticing her, but, oh, she did want that dress.

It was the most beautiful shade of pink.

Trish went back out into the main part of the store. Ian sat in a chair with two of the salesclerks hovering over him.

He looked up and saw her, his face covered with a surprised expression as he stood and walked toward her. "Are you finished?"

She gave him a wry smile. "Apparently."

She was about to draw him aside and ask the price of the dress when he grabbed her hand and started for the door, checking his watch.

"Good. Now you won't be late for your appointments."

Trish drew a blank. "What appointments?" She knew he had things to do, but she didn't.

"Hair, nails. You know, girly things." He smiled at her.

"But —" She'd never had her nails done, and she could wash her own hair.

He opened the door of the shop. "My treat. Consider it a bonus. You work too hard, and you need some time just for yourself."

She pulled him to a stop and stood on tiptoe so she could talk to him without being overheard. "Ian, there was no price tag on the dress. You need to check and see how much it was."

He bent toward her as if he was going to kiss her, then straightened and laughed at her surprised look. "Done already. Let's go." He took her arm.

Head spinning with the thought, she looked back over her shoulder. "But what about the dress?"

He nudged her out the door. "They'll deliver it to the hotel. Come on."

They emerged onto the busy sidewalk. What a contrast to the shop. Here it was all hustle and bustle and the smells and sounds of the city.

She felt as if she was in the middle of a wonderful dream. "Where are we going?" she asked as he took her by the hand.

"It's in the next block." He maneuvered them out into the flow of people, and they blended into the crowd surging along the sidewalk.

If she hadn't been with Ian she would have felt panicked by the crowds and noise. The city seemed to have its own pulse and energy.

They passed the sparkling windows of a jewelry store, filled with displays of beautiful rings, bracelets and necklaces. Trish's steps faltered as she was drawn to the beautiful sparkle of the gems.

Ian pulled her out of the crowd on the sidewalk and to a stop in front of the plate-glass windows. "Is there a woman alive that can walk past Tiffany's without slowing down?"

Tiffany's. Just the name conjured up such images, Trish thought as she stared in the window. "Everything is so beautiful."

She'd never had jewelry, not even a wedding ring. The truck had needed another repair the weekend she'd married, and they'd had no money for rings.

Ian smiled down at her. "Which do you like better? Yellow gold or platinum?"

She considered the rings on display. "Yellow I think. The diamonds look prettier against the gold."

He shrugged as if her opinion didn't matter. He'd probably just been making conversation, she thought.

He tugged on her hand. "We're late."

About a half block farther along Ian turned her into a doorway and opened a heavy etched-glass door. The interior reminded her of the dress shop but smelled even better.

A receptionist sat at a beautiful antique desk in front of more etched, frosted glass. Her hair and dress were both a rich shade of gray. She sprang to her feet and came around to greet them. "Mr. Miller. We've been expecting you."

Ian pulled Trish up beside him. "This is

Ms. Ryan. Michelle has the schedule."

"Of course. Ms. Ryan, if you'll follow me?"

Trish hung back. "Ian, how long will this take? I have to feed Emma."

"No problem. I'm going to get Sarah and Emma now. While you feed the baby, Sarah can get her nails done. Then Freddy will take them back to the hotel. I'll tell him to show them inside. The manager will make sure they get to the room. That sound okay to you?"

Okay? Trish was overwhelmed. He'd thought of everything. Sarah would be so excited.

Trish nodded as he bent down to brush her lips with a kiss. "You have fun."

In a daze she watched him stride out of the shop. Just as his feet hit the sidewalk, the car pulled up and Freddy jumped out to open the door.

Life for Ian Miller just seemed to fall into place so easily. She bit back a sigh. The man was so easy to love.

"Ms. Ryan?"

Trish turned and smiled at the receptionist.

"Follow me, please. We'll send your nanny back when she arrives."

Trish stifled another giggle. Her nanny.

Sarah was going to love this.

She was swept into a series of rooms where she was bundled into a white cotton robe.

Sarah arrived, and Trish fed Emma. Right on schedule, Freddy was there to collect Sarah and Emma.

Trish had a facial, her hair was cut and styled, then her nails and toenails groomed and painted. Finally a very chirpy little man wearing a purple satin shirt applied makeup to her face.

By the time she was finished it was almost six o'clock. She hardly recognized the woman in the mirror. She emerged from the salon to find Freddy waiting for her at the curb.

He opened the door for her with a flourish. "Straight back to the hotel, Ms. Ryan?"

She felt more and more like Cinderella. "Yes, straight back." She still needed to feed Emma and get dressed for the party.

They were back at the hotel before she had time to work herself up to a big worry about the party.

She hurried through the lobby and up in the elevator. Sarah popped off the bed when she opened the door and stood staring at her.

"Oh, my gosh, you look incredible." Emma lay in the middle of the bed.

Trish had been trying to avoid her image in any mirror. The woman who stared back was startling unfamiliar. "Too much?" She never wore makeup and didn't like the feel of it on her skin.

"It's totally phat."

"Is that good?"

Sarah rolled her eyes. "Yeah, it's good."

Emma heard Trish's voice and let out a squawk. Trish hurried over to her. "I have to feed her so I can get dressed. Did they find my dress?" The pink dress could always be returned.

"You mean the blue one you brought from home?"

Trish nodded as she settled down to feed Emma.

"No, thank goodness."

Trish looked up at the teenager. "Why do you say that?"

Sarah rolled her eyes. "Because it was really ugly," she said bluntly. "Your new one came. I sneaked a peek before I put it in the closet. It's much better. And the underwear is awesome."

Trish felt a guilty little thrill. She had been hoping the hotel wouldn't find the dress. Then a thought occurred to her.

224

"Oh no. I forgot about shoes."

"A box with a pair of shoes in it was delivered, too. They go with the dress."

Had Ian thought of shoes? Would a man think of something like that? Or did she have the clerk to thank? "Get them for me, will you, so I can see if they fit."

Sarah said, "Okay, and then I'll run you a bubble bath. There are some bath salts in there that smell like the apple orchard in spring."

Sarah went to the closet and returned with a shoe box. She pulled out a pair of high-heeled backless shoes. They were covered in fabric a shade darker than the dress and had gold embroidery all over them.

"Just like Cinderella," she said, dangling them from her fingers.

Trish looked at the shoes and sighed. They were beautiful. Her stomach was churning with a mixture of excitement and fear.

She just hoped she could get through the night without turning into a pumpkin.

Chapter Fourteen

Trish was dressed for the party and standing in the middle of the room waiting for Ian, her stomach churning with butterflies of the large variety. Sarah had assured her several times she looked great.

Trish wasn't so sure. All she knew was that she looked different. Should she take the word of a teenager? Sarah thought everything about this trip was awesome.

Emma was down for the night, and Sarah was curled up on one of the beds trying to decide what movie she wanted to watch and what to order for dinner from room service.

The party was going to be held in the hotel, so if Sarah needed her, all she had to do was call Ian's cell phone and Trish could come upstairs.

And, a little voice in Trish's head said, if she needed to escape the party, all she had to do was find an elevator.

Trish glanced at the clock. She couldn't decide if she wanted Ian to hurry up, or not to come at all.

She'd never been so nervous in her life.

Part of her wanted to go to the party, and part of her wanted to curl up beside Sarah and stay right here in the safety of the room.

At his knock on the adjoining door she said, "Come in."

He stepped into the room and her heart nearly stopped. Ian in a tuxedo was something to behold.

He was staring at her as if he had never seen her before. She had to work very hard not to squirm.

"Please turn around," he said in a solemn voice.

Oh, no, she thought as she turned slowly around, her stomach jumping with nerves. He doesn't like how I look. It was too much — the dress, the hair. What had made her think she could do this?

Slowly a smile spread over his face and he said very quietly, "You look beautiful."

As she stood there with him looking at her, for the first time in her life she *felt* beautiful. It was a rather startling feeling.

He held out his hand. "Ready?"

"Yes." She turned to say goodbye to Sarah and caught the teenager in an openmouthed stare as she looked at Ian. Trish knew exactly what she was feeling.

Sarah snapped her jaw closed and grinned at Trish. She waggled her hand and said, "You two have a good time."

Trish swallowed and nodded, then reached for Ian's hand and followed him to the door.

When they were alone in the elevator, she said, "Ian, thank you for today. It was wonderful."

He smiled down at her. He was doing a lot of that lately, and it made her heart thump.

"You deserve it. You work so hard. I want you to know how much I appreciate what you do."

She felt herself blushing. He laughed and took her other hand, holding both of hers. The warmth of his hands made her feel safe, and she started to relax.

As the elevator began to slow down he said, "Trish, I want to —"

The doors slid open before he could finish, and an older couple got on, leaving Trish wondering what he was about to say.

They got off on the floor above the lobby. Immediately people swarmed toward Ian. Trish shrank back at the onslaught.

Ian caught her hand and pulled her to his side. "Steady. This will calm down in a few minutes," he said as they moved into the ballroom.

Flashes from cameras made her see spots, and the people crowding in on all sides made her jumpy.

She didn't know what exactly she had expected, but not this. She'd thought the party would be a small gathering of people to celebrate his new book. But there were several hundred people in the fancy room, and it looked as if every one of them wanted to stand next to Ian. She held on to his hand as if it were a lifeline.

Ian motioned to an older woman who excused her way through the crowd around Ian. He introduced her as his editor's assistant.

"Allison, will you take Trish and get her something to drink?"

The woman smiled pleasantly and nodded. "Of course."

Ian squeezed her hand and bent down to talk to her. "Go with Allison and find our table. I'll be along shortly."

Reluctantly Trish let go of his hand and followed Allison across the room towards a bar manned by three men in white jackets.

The young assistant smiled at her. "Better?"

Trish sighed. "I didn't expect it to be so crowded."

Allison threw back her head and laughed. "Thank goodness it is. We don't do parties like this for most of our authors."

Trish glanced around the room. It was as ornate as the rest of the hotel. The round tables were set with crystal glasses and gold-rimmed china. There were copies of his new book at each place.

She'd always known Ian was important, but on the farm it had just been a concept. Here she was seeing the reality.

Huge blowups of his book cover and the photo they used on the dust jacket were placed around the walls, surrounded by beautiful arrangements of flowers.

Allison's voice broke in on her thoughts. "What do you want to drink?"

Trish rarely drank and had no idea what she wanted. "Do they have fruit juice?"

The bartender nodded to her and smiled. "I have grapefruit, orange or cranberry. I can send for anything else."

Trish was not going to make a special request. "Orange juice is fine."

Without hesitation Allison said, "And I'll have a martini. Two olives."

While they waited for their drinks

Allison eyed her appraisingly. "So, you take care of Ian at his farm."

Her speculating look made Trish uncomfortable. "Yes." She laughed nervously. "I came with the place when he bought it."

"Well, it must be a good place for him to write. I did a read on his most recent draft and it's the best he's ever done. The fastest, too."

She was so glad. She knew he'd been worried about his work. "He seems to like it there. At the farm."

Allison smiled. "I'll bet he does. Who knew? The urban Ian Miller out in the middle of nowhere. I wouldn't have believed it."

Trish accepted her tall glass of orange juice from the bartender with a nod of thanks and thought about what Allison had said as she followed the woman to a table.

She always thought of Ian belonging at the farm. But this was his life, too. The fancy hotel and the evening clothes, parties she could only dream of. This was Ian's world.

She looked across the room and saw him. Joyce stood by his side. She wore a very simple short black dress that looked striking on her. They made a handsome couple, both of them tall, sleek and chic.

Trish watched as Joyce deftly guided Ian out of the crowd and over to a tall, thin, gray-haired man.

Allison leaned forward and spoke to Trish in a conspiratorial tone. "He's the head book reviewer for the *New York Times*. Very important contact. Joyce takes good care of Ian," she said.

Trish wanted to ask Allison so many questions but couldn't bring herself to voice even one. It seemed like prying, and even though she wanted to in the worst way, she wouldn't invade Ian's privacy by asking personal questions of a woman she barely knew.

She watched as Ian finished speaking to the reviewer. He headed for the table where she sat, when Joyce took him by the arm and pulled him toward a group of people just coming in the door.

She felt Allison stiffen beside her and glanced at her.

Allison nodded toward the group Ian was speaking to. "Our competition," she said with a wry smile. "They've been trying to lure him away for two years."

Trish was surprised. "Why did you invite the competition?"

Allison laughed, but her voice held little humor. "They weren't on *our* guest list.

Joyce must have invited them. She's trying to get things stirred up. Again."

Ian shook hands with the people he'd been speaking to and pointed them in the direction of the bar.

Abruptly Allison stood up, drink in hand. "Excuse me, will you?"

Before Trish could even nod, she was gone.

Ian looked across the room and waved, then started in her direction. Once again Joyce caught up with him and pulled him to stop and talk to someone.

At this rate it would take him all night to get to the table, but Trish really didn't mind. She was having such fun just sitting and watching people mill about the room.

It was easy to spot the people who were important. They seemed to be the suns in their own little universes as people swirled around them.

The clerk at the shop had been right. Most of the women were dressed in black. People were beginning to make their way to the tables. It must be time to eat. Trish looked at the array of silverware and glasses and felt a moment of panic. There was so much on the table she wasn't sure which of the glasses and small plates belonged to her, and the last thing she wanted to do was embarrass Ian.

Her thoughts were interrupted by an older couple who arrived at the table and stood behind two of the chairs. They introduced themselves as Robert and Irene Evans. Trish smiled, but their names meant nothing to her.

Just as they took their seats, Ian arrived.

He greeted the couple warmly and then turned to Trish. "Robert was my first editor. He bought my first book."

Robert's blue eyes twinkled. "I retired on a high after that. You were the find of my career."

Ian laughed and slid into the chair beside Trish. "It worked out well for both of us."

He draped his hand over the back of her chair and ran a finger over the bare skin of her shoulder, sending a thrill over her skin. "You having a good time?"

Before she could answer, Joyce slipped into a chair across the table. "Ian, your place is here." She indicated the chair to her left.

For the first time Trish noticed there were name cards on the table.

Ian glanced at Joyce and shrugged. "I'm fine here." He picked up the card in front of him and passed it across the table.

"Allison can take my place," he said, and was caught up in a conversation with a woman who had settled in the chair on Ian's other side. He introduced her as his current editor.

Trish glanced up and caught Joyce's look of pure venom directed at her, as if she were personally responsible for spoiling the seating chart.

She looked away, grateful that the waiter arrived with a salad so she had something to do beyond avoiding looking across the table at Joyce. Out of the corner of her eye she watched and waited until Mrs. Evans picked up a fork, then copied her.

The ploy worked so well, she used it on all the courses.

All through the sumptuous dinner, Joyce kept jumping up and dragging people over to the table to speak to Ian. Trish had to hide her smile. It was if he was a royal sultan, holding court.

He did it so well, being the center of attention. For a man who worked in isolation, he was very good in crowds.

Trish finally began to relax, feeling as though she was holding her own. The conversation was light and friendly, and if she didn't look across the table at Joyce, she felt she fit in, more than she could have hoped.

Just as they were finishing dessert, Ian reached into his pocket and looked at the display on his cell phone. He flipped the phone open and listened for a minute, then said goodbye.

"Trish, that was Sarah. Emma's awake."

Trish put her napkin on the table and stood. Ian and Robert also came to their feet.

Trish smiled at everyone and said good-night.

Ian put his napkin on the table and said, "I'll walk you up."

Joyce came to her feet like a shot and said, "Ian, you're having after-dinner drinks with Conrad Bertles."

Ian groaned under his breath. "I forgot."

Joyce looked ready to explode.

Trish said quickly, "I can go up on my own." She didn't want to end such a perfect evening with Joyce creating a scene.

Ian looked from Joyce to Trish and nodded reluctantly. "I'll see you later."

As she left the room she loved the fact that he'd wanted her to stay. All in all, she felt as if she'd held her own at the party. She'd met important people, had some nice conversations and used the right utensils. Blending into Ian's world hadn't been nearly as difficult as she'd imagined.

Trish reached the elevator just as the ornate clock tucked into a niche on the terrace level chimed midnight.

She'd had fun at the party, but like Cinderella it was time to end the fairy-tale evening.

Ian had missed Trish after she left the Terrace Room. If he hadn't been meeting Conrad to discuss the possibilities of adopting Emma and all it involved, he would have followed her.

"Ian?"

He realized he hadn't been paying the least bit of attention to his attorney.

"I asked if you've set a wedding date? We can start the adoption procedure as soon as you are married."

"No. I haven't asked her yet."

He smiled. "What are your chances?"

Ian was pretty sure of Trish, but he was still nervous. "Pretty good, I think."

His attorney nodded. "Good planning. Get all the details ironed out. We can talk about a prenup when you come in on Tuesday."

Ian shrugged. He didn't need a prenup. He knew Trish well enough to know how fiercely loyal she was. If she agreed to marry him, it would be forever.

Strangely, the thought of committing to a forever relationship in the past had never occurred to him.

Now it felt just right.

Chapter Fifteen

Trish was sitting up in bed early in the morning, nursing Emma and savoring memories of her fairy-tale evening. Sarah was still fast asleep in the other bed.

A knock sounded on the adjoining door.

"Come in," she called quietly.

Ian started into the room, then halted and averted his eyes. "I, uh, wondered if you wanted me to order you breakfast."

She looked over at him and noticed his discomfort. She pulled the sheet up to cover the baby and her bare breast, amused that a man as worldly as Ian was embarrassed by something so natural.

"We can wait. Sarah will be up soon."

"I won't be eating with you. I have some business to attend to that came up last night."

He seemed distracted. Trish wondered whether it was the fact she was feeding Emma or something else. She was disappointed they wouldn't be eating together.

"I can order when we're ready. When will you be back?" She would love to do some more sight-seeing with him before they all headed back to the farm.

"I'm staying for a day or two. Freddy will take you back as soon as you eat and get packed up." He still wasn't making eye contact, and Trish got an uneasy feeling.

Why was he sending her home? Had she done something last night that had embarrassed him? Something she wasn't even aware of?

"Ian, is something wrong?"

He finally looked up at her and flushed. "No," he said hurriedly. "Not at all."

He was acting very strange. She wanted to ask him what was keeping him in New York, but it was none of her business. She immediately thought of Joyce, and it upset her.

Trying to tamp down her uneasiness, she glanced at the clock beside the bed and calculated how much time they would need. "We can be ready in two hours."

"Just call the front desk when your bags are ready and they will come up and get them. Freddy will be out front."

He started across the room toward her, smiling, and she felt better.

Sarah stirred and sat up, yawning and rubbing her eyes. Ian stopped where he was, looking awkward and uncomfortable and very much unlike himself. He shoved his hands in his pockets and said, "Well, I'll see you back at the farm. Probably Tuesday afternoon."

Tuesday sounded so far away. She wanted to get out of bed and give him a hug and kiss, but her nightgown was unbuttoned halfway to her waist, she was still feeding Emma and there was a teenager in the next bed, watching them.

"Well," she said, "goodbye. We'll see you back at the farm."

He stood, hesitating for a moment, then nodded. "See you Tuesday."

He turned and disappeared back into his room.

Sarah yawned again. "Mr. Miller isn't coming back with us?"

"No. He has business here. We'll go as soon as we get packed up."

Sarah flopped back on the bed, hugging herself. "I still can't believe we're in New York City. At the Plaza. Wait till I see everyone at school tomorrow. They'll be so jealous!"

Trish smiled at the teenager. "I imagine you did have the best weekend of anyone you know."

Sarah rolled to her side and propped her head on one hand. "Tell me about the party again. What did you have for dinner?"

Trish fought down her feelings of disappointment and niggling thoughts that Ian was holding something back, and related the whole evening again to Sarah, right down to the dessert that looked like a chocolate oyster shell filled with chocolate mousse floating on a puddle of rich sweet cream laced with raspberry sauce.

On Monday afternoon Trish got so lonely with Ian gone she put Emma in her snuggle pack and walked down to see the progress on the stone farmhouse.

The workers had finished the roof installation and the new windows. She heard hammering and the whir of a power saw from inside and peeked in the door. The smell of sawdust hung in the air. The insulation and wiring were up, and inside walls were finished on two sides. Cabinets under the small counter space in the kitchen area had been installed. She hardly recognized the place.

The two workers looked up and nodded, but she waved and retreated out the door so as not to disturb their work.

When she turned to go to the barn to feed Max, she saw a car coming up the drive and her heart leaped. Ian was home early.

She started toward the house as the car pulled to the front. She could taste the disappointment when she realized it was Joyce and not Ian who had arrived.

Joyce was emerging from her car when Trish got to the front door. Could it be possible that Joyce didn't know Ian had stayed in New York? She felt silly that she'd worried about them there together.

"Hello, Trish. That's so . . . cute." She pointed at Emma in the snug pack. "The way you haul that baby around with you," Joyce said with her usual dismissive tone.

Trish knew Joyce didn't think anything about her was *cute*. At least she'd gotten her name right.

With that snide greeting, she turned her back on Trish and headed for the front door. "Ian sent me for his black suit and some other things he needs," she said over her shoulder. "He forgot about the tickets tonight for a show."

Trish felt a little ill. They were going out tonight, to a show.

She stopped on the threshold and smiled at Trish. "I'll tell you, it will be so much easier after we move into the New York apartment. These trips up here into the wilderness are so tedious." She turned and stepped into the house.

Trish stopped dead and had to struggle to draw in a breath. Ian was moving back to New York? With Joyce? She waited until she caught her bearings, then followed Joyce into the house and up the stairs.

She must have misheard. Ian loved the farm. And he was fond of her. He'd tell her if he was going to leave.

Wouldn't he?

A little voice inside her head whispered to her that he might be fond of her, but she wasn't the kind of woman he would need. He wouldn't ever fall in love with her.

She wasn't lovable. Hadn't she gotten the message? Her parents wouldn't have abandoned her if she was lovable. Someone would have adopted her if she was lovable.

All the hurt and pain of being left behind rushed at her, choking her.

She stood in the doorway to Ian's room trying to get herself under control. She would not break down in front of this woman.

She watched Joyce select a suit and several shirts from the closet. As she smoothed her immaculately manicured hand over the fabric of his suit, Trish saw the diamond on the third finger of her left hand.

Trish wondered vaguely why she didn't double over with the pain. "Do you need me for anything else?"

Joyce looked up as if she was surprised to see Trish standing there. "Why, no. I have everything under control."

Trish turned to go downstairs, sure that Joyce was right. She did have everything under control. And Trish had nothing.

Trish couldn't stay in the house. She was afraid she was going to cry, and all she had left was her pride. She'd be darned if she would let Joyce see how upset she was.

She headed down to the barn and curled up on a bale of hay beside Max's stall, hugging Emma to her chest.

Max hung his head over the stall door and whickered a greeting to her. She heard Joyce's car pull away, and finally she allowed herself to lose control. She cried into the sleeping baby's soft curls until she felt drained.

She pulled a corner of the blanket tucked around Emma up and dried her face. Thank goodness she hadn't made a fool of herself by telling Ian she was in love with him.

She heard the sound of someone coming

up the drive and cringed. If it was Joyce, she was going to hide in the barn. She simply couldn't face that woman again.

She dragged herself to her feet and peered out toward the house. It wasn't Joyce, it was an older man getting out of an old truck. He stood beside his vehicle and gave the house a long look, then turned and looked at the barn, then past that to the stone house.

She gave her eyes a final wipe and stepped out into the thin winter sunlight. "May I help you?"

"Mrs. Miller?"

Tears welled up and she forced them back. "My name is Trish. Trish Ryan."

He held out a callused hand. "Jack Travers. I come to see about the caretaker job."

Trish faltered. "The job?"

"Yeah, I answered the ad Mr. Miller's property manager placed. Is Mr. Miller here?"

Numbly she said, "No, he's still in New York. He'll be home tomorrow."

Mr. Travers pointed to the stone house. Her home. "That the caretaker's place?"

Trish nodded.

"Mind if I take a look? I can come back on Thursday and talk to Mr. Miller."

Wooden with grief and fear, she forced the words out. "That would be fine." Abruptly she turned and headed for the house before she lost control again.

If he had questions, he'd have to talk to Ian.

After she was gone.

There was no way she could stay here now. When Joyce came here with Ian, Trish had no doubt she would sleep in his bed. There was no way she could stay on as the housekeeper in the same house where Ian was sleeping with another woman.

When Ian had come to live at Blacksmith Farm, she'd been so afraid of being fired and losing her home. To her it had been the worst thing that could happen.

Now she realized how wrong she'd been.

She could find another home.

She'd lost her heart. And that she couldn't replace.

Chapter Sixteen

"What do you mean you can't find her?" Ian shouted into the telephone at the investigator as he paced the braided rug in the farm's great room.

He cursed the fact that he'd let Joyce make appointments for television and radio appearances that had kept him in New York an extra two days.

He stuck his hand in his pocket and fingered the diamond ring he'd bought for Trish in New York.

He'd called Trish from New York and left messages when she hadn't answered the phone. He'd pictured her down in the barn with Max, or in town doing errands.

He should have come back here right away when he didn't reach her. He'd been so busy he hadn't asked her to call back. He'd just told her he was staying some extra days.

He rubbed his hand across the stubble on his jaw. Something had happened. He had no idea what, but something had driven her from the farm.

The investigator's patient voice broke into his thoughts. "I didn't say I couldn't, I said it would take time."

The investigator Ian had hired was keeping his cool — more than Ian could say for himself. He poured another cup of coffee. He'd been existing on coffee for the past twenty-four hours, and his nerves were shot.

Ian looked at the note from Trish as the investigator kept talking.

"She doesn't use credit cards, she doesn't have a bank account or a cell phone, and as far as we know, she doesn't have a job. Yet."

The man had been working, but Ian wanted more. He wanted Trish. All Ian had been able to tell the investigator was that Trish had called his property manager and asked for her final check.

He'd checked with Sarah and her mother, and they didn't know where Trish had gone, either.

"As soon as she gets a job or applies for financial aid, we'll find her."

Ian thanked the man and hung up. He continued to stare at the note he'd read a hundred times, trying to figure out why she'd gone.

All it said was she was quitting, there

was a man named Travers who was taking
the caretaker's job and would look after
the animals. When she found a place to
live she'd contact him about Max, the cat
and the dog.

She'd signed her name, then added a
congratulations, and that she hoped he'd
be happy.

Happy? How could he be happy without
her?

Congratulations for what? Surely that
was significant, but he had no idea what
she was talking about. And how did she
think he could be happy if she wasn't at
the farm?

He depended on her. He looked forward
to seeing her every morning.

He loved her.

Ian sat down abruptly at the kitchen
table.

He loved her. And Emma. Funny that
the thought hadn't occurred to him while
he'd been discussing prenuptials and adoption with his attorney.

He felt like an idiot. Is that why she left?
He didn't think so. Somehow that couldn't
be the reason. There was the cryptic congratulations at the end of her note that had
to be the key.

He heard a vehicle pulling up to the

house and dropped the note and his coffee onto the table.

He raced out the front door and was disappointed to see an old truck coming up the driveway. A man stepped out. "Are you Mr. Miller?"

"Yes," Ian practically yelled at him. "Did you come about Trish Ryan?"

The man gave him a startled look. "No. I came about the caretaker's job. My name is Travers."

Ian remembered a message from the property manager saying he'd found a caretaker. "Mr. Travers, did you meet Ms. Ryan?"

The older man smiled. "Sure did. Cute little thing. Gave her and the baby a ride to town."

Ian's heart leaped. "When?"

"Day before yesterday. Early in the morning. She called and said I had the job and she needed some help."

Impatient, Ian barked, "Where did you take her?"

Travers eyed him suspiciously, and for a moment Ian was afraid he wasn't going to answer.

"Let her off at that motel on the highway, just before you get to that miniature golf course with all them big plaster animals."

Ian struggled to get hold of his emotions. He took a deep breath and in a calmer voice he asked, "Did she say why she was leaving?"

"Can't say that she did. She was pretty quiet." Travers took off his cap and scratched his balding head. "I could tell something was bothering her, but it wasn't my business. Made me promise I'd stop by and feed the animals."

"Thanks. That helps."

"Mind if I take a look at the stone house before I take care of the critters?"

"No, go ahead," Ian said distractedly as he went into the house to call the investigator back.

He gave the man the information Mr. Travers had told him, and then told the investigator he was on his way to the motel.

"Miller, wait. Why don't you let me check it out and see if she's there. He dropped her off, but that doesn't mean she's staying at that motel."

Ian knew it was the reasonable thing to do, but the inaction was driving him crazy. As he fought with himself, the investigator said, "I can check and get back to you in a few minutes. Sit tight and I'll call."

Sit tight? He was so agitated he couldn't sit at all. "Call me on my cell phone."

Two minutes later his telephone rang. It was the investigator.

"She was at the motel for two nights. Took a cab this morning but asked them to store her belongings until she came for them. She picked her things up this afternoon, also by cab. She didn't have the baby with her when she came back, and she mentioned she'd found a job, so she couldn't have gone very far. Now that we have a place to start, I should be able to find her pretty quickly."

"Okay. You call me if you find *anything.*" Where would she have left Emma? Was she staying with a friend? He didn't remember her ever mentioning having friends in town.

The investigator's voice broke in on his thoughts. "Yes, sir. We'll be in touch."

Ian opened the front door, and the dog and cat were sitting on the porch. They both stared at him as if to ask where Trish was. "I don't know!" he yelled at the two animals, then felt like an idiot.

He wandered around the house for an hour until his cell phone rang again. He checked the caller ID. When he saw it was Joyce he let his voice mail pick up. He didn't want to talk business and he knew any conversation with her now would only annoy him.

Two minutes later the phone rang again and it was the investigator.

"We located Ms. Ryan."

He slumped in relief. "Where?"

"She was hired yesterday at the Sunny Vale Retirement Home. It's not far from the motel."

"Did you find out where she's living?"

"Apparently on the premises at Sunny Vale. They have a few efficiency units they reserve for the night shift workers."

Ian closed his eyes in relief. She was safe and still nearby.

"Do you want me to make contact with Ms. Ryan?"

Ian cleared his throat. "No. Give me the address and I'll go."

The investigator gave him the address, and Ian thanked the man as he took the stairs two at a time. He needed to shower and shave and change out of the clothes he'd been in for two days.

He was ready to go in under half an hour. He headed out to his car and met Travers in the driveway.

"Okay with you, Mr. Miller, if I move in on Saturday?"

Ian was anxious to get going. He didn't have time for conversation. He said, "The house isn't ready."

Travers planted his feet and shot Ian a stubborn look. "Close. I can save you some by doing the painting. The fellows working on the place said they don't do painting."

Ian didn't care, he just wanted to find Trish. "Sure. Okay. Saturday, then." He got in his car and headed into town as dusk fell.

Unfamiliar with the area, he missed the last turnoff before the retirement home and had to double back. Frustrated, he slowed down and made the turn into the parking lot.

He stepped out of his car in front of a sprawl of ugly yellow cinder-block buildings with brown trim.

He strode up the front walk and into a hot, stuffy reception area paneled in fake wood. There was a door behind the desk, and one on either side. A woman with steel-gray hair sat behind the desk.

The place smelled like macaroni and cheese with a heavy overlay of disinfectant.

She gave him a fake smile. "May I help you?"

"I'm looking for Trish Ryan."

The woman looked down at a printed page on the desktop and frowned. "We don't have a resident by that name."

He ran his hand through his hair and

shook his head. "She works here. She was just hired."

She eyed him suspiciously, then glanced down at another piece of paper before looking back up at him. "I can't give out that information. Data about our employees is confidential."

Frustration made Ian wanted to shout at the woman, but he knew it wouldn't help the situation. Instead he forced a smile and said, "My name is Ian Miller. Ms. Ryan worked for me until a few days ago. I need to give her her final check."

She peeked into a folder on the desk. "She gave you as a reference." The woman's expression softened somewhat. "I'll need to verify you are who you say you are."

Ian dug his driver's license out of his wallet and handed it over. She pursed her lips and shook her head. Hurriedly he said, "That's my old address." He gave her the address for the farm.

She nodded, apparently satisfied. "You can leave the check with me. I'll see she gets it."

Ian wanted to dive across the desk and throttle the woman. He struggled to keep his voice calm. "There is some unfinished business. I really need to talk with her."

She hesitated, eyeing him, then said stiffly, "Ms. Ryan has just started her shift."

"This will only take a minute," he reassured her.

"Let me see if I can locate her." Ian felt a rush of relief as she dialed a telephone. After a short conversation with the person on the other end of the line, she asked that Trish come to the front desk.

She hung up and stood at her desk. "Ms. Ryan will be right out. I will go cover for her. Please wait here." She disappeared through the door behind the desk.

Ian paced the speckled tile floor as he waited for Trish, keeping his eye on the door the receptionist had gone through. He glanced at his watch and realized it was February fourteenth. Valentine's Day. He'd always thought the holiday was silly, but suddenly he wished he'd brought roses and a big heart-shaped box of chocolates.

Finally the door to his left opened and Trish stood there, looking as if she was poised for flight. Behind her he could see a dining hall filled with seniors having supper.

Her face was very pale and she looked as if she'd lost weight. "Hello, Ian. What are you doing here?"

"What am I doing here? What are you doing here?" He was trying to keep his voice at a reasonable level.

She made a shushing sound and looked over her shoulder. "Stop talking so loudly. You'll agitate the residents." She stepped into the reception area and let the door swing closed behind her.

"Where's Emma?" he demanded.

Trish had her arms crossed over her stomach. "In the dining room being spoiled by several ladies who don't see enough of their great-grandchildren."

She'd left her with strangers? "Are they, you know, okay to take care of her?"

She drew herself up at his question. "Do you think I'd leave her with someone who wasn't okay?"

"No, of course not." He backpedaled at the fire in her eyes.

She stared at him for a moment, then said, "Mrs. Sterns said you had a check for me. I already picked up my check."

He ran his hand through his hair again, trying to calm down. "I lied. The woman wasn't going to tell me if you were here. Why did you leave the farm?" he demanded.

Her eyes welled up. "You really weren't going to need a housekeeper full-time while you were living in New York."

What was she talking about? "I'm not living in New York." He took a step toward her and she backed up against the door.

A single tear trickled down her cheek. "But you will be."

Why did she think he was moving to New York? Everything he'd ever wanted was at Blacksmith Farm. "Who told you that?"

"Joyce. When she came to get your suit on Monday, she said you were looking for an apartment."

His suit? An apartment? This conversation was making no sense. "Joyce came to the farm?" That was news to him.

Trish nodded, and another tear followed the first. She wiped her face with the heel of her hand.

What the heck was going on? "And said I was moving to New York?"

She nodded again.

"Perhaps you misunderstood —"

"No!" Trish said fiercely. "She made it very clear the two of you were moving in together."

Ian's mouth fell open. Joyce was gutsy and pushy, but this was too much. "She lied to you."

"Did she? Are you sleeping with her?"

Ian squirmed, wishing he'd been more open about his former relationship with Joyce. "We had an affair. It's been over since well before I met you."

Trish narrowed her eyes and skewered him with a look. "Are you sure?"

Indignant, he said, "Of course I'm sure." He had *never* lied to her.

She threw her hands up in a gesture of frustration. "Well, apparently Joyce isn't!"

He stared at her. She was jealous. She hadn't left because she didn't care for him. He felt so giddy he closed his eyes for a second and savored the feeling of relief.

When he opened his eyes again he found she'd turned to go back through the door. He grabbed her arm and swung her around.

"Trish, it's over with Joyce. Has been for a long time. We weren't in love, it was just . . ." He searched for the right word. "Convenient."

He hated the way that sounded, and from her reaction, she did, too.

She tried to jerk away and he held tight, desperate to make her listen. "I want you to come back. I need you."

She shook her head, her chin tucked down against her chest.

This was not going well at all. How

could he be so good with words on paper and so bad with her?

Desperation swamped him and he caught her other arm, bringing her around to face him. "Trish, I want you at the farm. I miss you and Emma. I need you."

She swallowed, and her voice came out sad and low. "Ian, I don't think I can work there anymore."

"Why not?" Hadn't he just told her how much he needed her?

She squirmed in his grasp and wouldn't look him in the eye. "Because."

He let go of her arm and tipped her chin up so he could see her face. Her face was glassy with tears. "That's not an answer. Besides, I don't want you to work there."

She blinked back more tears. "What *do* you want?"

He smiled at the spunk in her voice, then took a deep breath for courage and said the words he'd never said to anyone. "I love you. I want you there, with me."

She looked at him, dumbfounded, then a sad expression crossed her face. "But, Ian, I don't belong in your world."

He pulled her into his arms. "Oh, Trish, you *are* my world."

But for how long? she wondered, nestled against the strong warmth of his chest.

How much time would it take for him to see she didn't belong with him? Or deserve him, a little voice in her head said.

She'd had enough abandonment to last her a lifetime, she thought, even as she savored the feel of his arms around her. She had to consider Emma, too. What kind of example would it set for her daughter if she lived with Ian?

"Trish." His impatient voice pulled her out of her thoughts. She stepped back and broke the embrace, knowing it would be the last one she'd have with him.

Now he was angry with her again.

"Marry me." He pulled a ring out of his pocket, then scooped up her left hand and slid the ring on her third finger.

Stunned, she didn't even look at the ring. Her eyes were glued on his face. "What?"

"Was that so hard to understand? I said I want you to marry me," he said, his chin jutted out and his shoulders squared as if he were ready for a fight.

"No." Actually she didn't understand. Then she said, "Yes," and shook her head, thoroughly confused. Why would he want to marry her?

He bounced on the balls of his feet and shoved his hands in his pockets. "Well, which is it? Yes or no?"

He wasn't angry, she realized, he was scared, and he was trying to look brave.

Her heart gave a big lurch, and a curl of warmth that felt like hope started in her chest. "Why?" she asked. "Why do you want me to marry you?"

He yanked his hands out of his pockets and threw them up in a gesture of exasperation. "I told you. I love you. I've never said that before. To anyone."

She stared at him. Maybe he really did love her. "Since when? How long?" She needed to know. Perhaps he'd think it wasn't important, but she wanted to know. As far as she knew, no one had ever loved her.

He ran a hand through his hair. "Exactly? I don't know." Then he closed his eyes again and exhaled noisily. "In the barn."

They'd been in the barn several times. "Which time?"

He shook his head and looked resigned. "The first time. You'd snuck out to feed Max. Before I knew about him."

He'd loved her before she'd fallen in love with him. For some reason that was very special to her. Suddenly a future with him seemed possible.

"Oh, Ian," she sighed, hope and want and dreams combining into a feeling of rightness.

"Trish, you're killing me here." He reeled her back in and cradled her against his chest. "Say yes," he said into her hair. "For heaven's sake, put me out of my misery and say yes."

She tipped her head back and stared at his beautiful face. For the first time she could remember, she felt confident about her future. "Yes," she whispered.

He used one hand to wipe the tears off her cheeks. "Louder. So the world can hear it."

"Yes!" She threw her arms around him and pulled his head down so she could kiss him.

He broke the kiss and said, "Let's go get Emma and go home."

She sighed in his arms, feeling cherished.

"Home. Yes, let's go home."